BOTTLE RABBIT

ff

BOTTLE
RABBIT

Bernard McCabe

illustrated by
Axel Scheffler

faber and faber

LONDON · BOSTON

First published in 1988
by Faber and Faber Limited
3 Queen Square London WC1N 3AU

Photoset by Parker Typesetting Service Leicester
Printed in Great Britain by
Mackays of Chatham Ltd Kent

British Library Cataloguing in Publication Data

McCabe, Bernard
Bottle Rabbit.
I. Title   II. Scheffler, Axel
823'.914[J]   PZ7
ISBN 0-571-14978-2

For Kate, John, Matthew, Louisa,
Daniel, Anne, Alexander and Peter

And in memory of Lucy

Contents

Bottle Rabbit Meets the Crad

Charlie's curvy old pipe puffed rich smoke. Fred's battered straw hat tilted over his broad forehead. A blue sky shone above their nodding heads. Behind their broad brown backs the red-and-white cart bumped and jumped over the cobblestones and their passenger bounced about on the cart bench. All the time he laughed and sang. You couldn't ask for a friendlier or nicer-looking young animal. A taut woolly black body, white buttons up his front, comfortable ears and paws, and in the middle of his plump stomach two big white pockets. In the right-hand one, the bulgier one, his Magic Bottle. Who was he? The Bottle Rabbit, of course, off on an outing.

Fred and Charlie's powerful knees smartly rose and fell as their great furred hooves struck sparks from the cobblestones. The two handsome, muscular Clydesdales loved this kind of outing with their young friend, and had left their neat wooden cabin bright and early that morning.

Soon they swung into the woods on a green path and rumbled along much more quietly, their hooves thud-thudding on the grass. The Bottle Rabbit leant back happily to watch the sky through the green and black intertwining branches.

Fred and Charlie knew exactly where to stop first. It was beside the biggest tree in a grove of fine beeches.

'Do you think this is the right tree?' asked the Bottle Rabbit.

'Oh, yes, I should think so. Don't you think so, Charlie?' rumbled Fred slowly. Charlie took his pipe out of his mouth, looked at it carefully, grinned and said nothing. So the Bottle Rabbit leapt out of the cart, scampered up to the tree and, making a fist out of his paw, knocked on it three times as hard as he could. Paw on wood made a soft thud. *A door opened in the tree.* And standing there was a startlingly beautiful white cat, smiling and twirling her tail.

'Emily, Emily, Fred and Charlie and I are going on an outing; it's to be a picnic. Can you come? *Please* come,' said the Bottle Rabbit. The cat nodded and smiled and without a word slipped back into her tree. It was her *house* really. You could see a dining-room and a drawing-room with fireplaces, plates on the wall, buckets of coal, teapots and family portraits.

'I'm ready,' said Emily.

'Good. Hurry up and get into the cart,' said the Bottle Rabbit. So Emily hopped up beside him on the bench and off they went, rumbling on through the leafy woods.

3

After a long and enjoyable drive they trundled up to a quiet place with a stream rippling between mossy banks, several fallen trees, and a shiny rock.

'The perfect spot. Right, Charlie?' grunted Fred. Charlie nodded and they stopped.

All four animals spread out blankets and a white linen table-cloth, and Fred opened up the big straw picnic baskets. Then all settled down for lunch. There

were ham sandwiches, egg sandwiches, cheese-and-pickle sandwiches, pickled eggs, cold sausages, a pork pie, a steak-and-kidney pie, several sorts of chutney, a little pot of spiced beans, some tomatoes and radishes, lemonade, ginger beer, herb beer and two little old oaken casks of bitter beer for Fred and Charlie. Also plenty of cherries and also a lot of lemons, mostly for Fred, who liked to eat them whole in one big bite. Everybody ate a lot and drank quite a bit. Then Fred and Charlie settled down for a little snooze.

'Let's go for a walk, Emily.'

'Yes, let's.'

And paw in paw the Bottle Rabbit and Emily walked off into the woods. Looking back for a moment they caught a glimpse of Fred and Charlie stretched peacefully between the little beer-barrels. 'Enjoy yourselves,' muttered Fred, waving a kindly hoof. Charlie gave a sort of smiling snore. They wandered off some way into the quiet woods.

All seemed peaceful and friendly, when suddenly, almost in a flash, a dark shadow hung over them. It was as if a thundercloud had raced across the sun.

'Crark, Crark, Crark. What you doin' 'ere? Crark. What's that you got in your pocket, Rabbit? Crark. Lemme see,' called a harsh voice.

Emily's paw tightened in the Bottle Rabbit's as they looked up and saw two huge gnarled claws gripping the thickest branch of an elm tree above them. The claws were ribbed and twisted, with broken toenails. Above the toes stretched raggy tree-trunk legs, yellow and black and pale, and above them a great ragged rough body and a head with little hectic red eyes blinking and blinking, and an enormous beak. It was the pestilent Crad.

'Know me now, do yer?' said the Crad.

'Yes, sir, we do, sir,' both animals said nervously and hurriedly.

'Well, what's in yer pocket, rabbit? I bin 'earing about you. Show us what yer got.'

So the Bottle Rabbit worriedly pulled out his little dark green Bottle.

'Crark, Crark, Crark,' went the Crad. 'So that's your famous Bottle, is it? Doesn't look like much to me. Just a bit of piddlin' dark green glass, that's all it is.'

'Oh, but you can do *hundreds* of different things with it if you pongle it,' cried the young Rabbit eagerly, as he slipped the Bottle back into his pocket. 'You can arrange to fly just about anywhere straight off with the

Six Blue Hares or the Twelve Mice, depending, or it can get you sandwiches and buns and . . .' Here he broke off as he felt Emily's delicate little white paw tugging at his black one.

But the Crad's little red eyes blinked faster and faster. 'Ponglin'. Yerss. I knew there was *some* trick to it more than what the Merritt said. Stands to reason.'

The Crad gave a clumsy sort of half-flap of wing, half-jump, and came thumping down next to them under the tree. He didn't look quite so big now, but still pretty big, and *very* ugly, and a bit smelly too, like old breadcrumby waistcoats mixed with stale water in flower vases. His little red eyes were glistening.

'Listen. I got a damn big bag of gold coins 'ere. You could buy anything with it. I'll give yer the whole bloomin' lot if you'll hand over that Bottle.'

And he held open a large black soft-leather bag. The Bottle Rabbit and Emily stared into it and their eyes nearly popped out with surprise. It was full of bright gold coins, bright and new and thick. Jangling and clinking, they were so bright they shone red as well as gold.

The Bottle Rabbit sighed with happiness. He was not afraid of the Crad any more, now that he was down on the ground with a bagful of money; and having Emily standing firmly next to him, paw in paw, was a help too. But he wanted those gold coins. He loved gold coins. And he quickly pulled the Bottle out of his pocket again.

Emily didn't like this at all.

'Bottle Rabbit, dear Bottle Rabbit,' she whispered, 'think what you are doing. Think. This is your wonderful Bottle. Don't give it away for a mere heap of gold.' She stroked his paw. 'Can gold bring you happiness?' murmured Emily.

6

'Yes. It can. I love it,' said the Bottle Rabbit loudly. 'Here, Crad. Take the Bottle. Just be sure to give me the whole bagful of gold.'

'Crark, Crark, Crark.' Quick as a flash the Crad clasped the Bottle to his ragged black breast, flung the soft leather bag at the Rabbit, and with a couple of dusty flaps was off into the air.

Emily stared after him, a tear rolling down her white cheek. The Bottle Rabbit plunged his paws into his gold.

'Look! Look! Listen, Emily!' His woolly paws plunged and plunged into the glittering clinking heaps.

7

'There's *hundreds* of them. I can buy anything I want.'

'But the Bottle, Bottle Rabbit, the Bottle. *How* could you give it away? You know you . . .'

Emily suddenly stopped and stared. The poor young animal was whimpering. His paws still moved in the Crad's black bag, but the only sound now was a dry rustle, and the only colour a dusty brown.

All was suddenly quiet. Then –

8

'Emily, it's *leaves*. It's just old dead *leaves*,' and the poor Rabbit stood there with his back bent in misery while one huge tear rolled down his cheek, and then another.

'And I've lost my Bottle. Oh, what a fool I've been. It wasn't gold at all,' he cried. The plump woolly young animal wept heart-rendingly.

Somehow the Crad had tricked him.

'Quick. Let's follow him,' said Emily, and darted off into the woods in the direction the Crad had taken. The Bottle Rabbit stumbled after her. But what chance had they? The Crad was half a mile away by now. In the woods everything had gone completely still. In the dead silence they could just hear the distant creaking of the Crad's dry wings, and a faint echo of his horrible Crark, Crark.

This was a very bad time for both animals, because soon they saw that, as well as everything else, they were lost. They had simply no idea how to find their trusty, strong old horse-friends, Fred and Charlie. It had gone a bit cold and windy. A black cloud had carried the sun away. Emily shivered and the Bottle Rabbit put his paw round her shoulders to keep her warm. He was beginning to feel quite frightened but bravely stood up straight and said, 'Don't worry, Emily, we'll find a way,' just as Emily, who was also feeling frightened, bravely said, 'Don't worry, Bottle Rabbit, we'll get home somehow.' This made them both laugh and cheered them up a bit.

Better still, they now heard a high soft whistling call from the sky, and in a few seconds down swooped a huge wonderful golden bird. It was the Golden Eagle.

9

And better again, on his back, munching cake, was the
Golden Baker, the Golden Eagle's close friend.
 'Jump on. No time. Let's move. Off.'

And away they soared. The Golden Eagle always
spoke like that. He could see 1,000 miles in any direction from high up. As they tore through the air, the
Golden Eagle's great wings beating slowly and
strongly, the Baker explained that the two worried
horses were wondering what had happened and had
asked them to help. Emily told the whole story – Crad,
money, Bottle, leaves – to the Golden Baker. The
Bottle Rabbit, a bit embarrassed, kept looking away
and humming bits of tunes he knew. But the Baker

10

nodded kindly and spoke a few words close to the Golden Eagle's ear. The Eagle half-turned his noble and beautiful head, nodded, and started to make wide circling swings over the forest below, his brilliant great eyes staring and staring.

'Looking for the Crad,' muttered the Golden Baker, 'and by golly, he's got him. There he is. Got 'im!'

He wiped his lips and pointed down into a clearing in the woods, and there sure enough they could see the bald dirty pink patch on the top of the Crad's pear-shaped head. From where they were, he seemed to be sneezing.

The Golden Eagle made a silent swoop and landed silently a hundred yards behind the Crad's back.

'Quiet. Look. Listen. Don't speak or move. Just look.'

They all crept a little nearer and stared and listened. The Crad was holding up the Bottle. His bony face twisted with anger as he clacked his heavy beak against the top of the Bottle, and hunched his tattered shoulders trying to pongle.

'PONGLE. Confound this Bottle. PONGLE. The thing isn't working. PONGLE. Curse this bottle. PON-GLE. Where's that damn Rabbit? PONGLE!'

It was quite funny to see, really, and even the Bottle Rabbit's tear-stained face had a bit of a grin on it now.

The Baker and the Eagle were discussing the situation. 'Case for Sam. Yes. Get the Bear,' said the Golden Eagle and flew off like a shot. The Crad went on pongling and cursing and staring into the Bottle. The three friends sat quietly under a tree to wait, and the Golden Baker handed round some excellent currant cake and fizzy drink from a small knapsack.

11

Fifteen minutes later the ground began to tremble.

THUD, pause, THUD, pause, THUD, pause. They looked at one another. What could it be? The Bottle Rabbit guessed first, and jumped to his feet excitedly.

'It's Sam. It's Sam the Bear,' he said in a happy whisper. 'I'm sure it's Sam. Sam's coming.'

And he was right. The thuds got closer and closer and louder and louder. Sam the Bear, one of the Bottle Rabbit's dearest friends, was pounding towards him through the forest. His great towering body and his huge heavy legs, black and huge, covered yards and yards at a stride. The Crad suddenly stopped pongling and looked fearfully over his shoulder. Sam's enormous eyes, usually kindly but now very stern, were set on the Crad as he crouched trembling before him with the Bottle shaking in his claw.

Sam was very strong, but also very gentle. He did not hurt the Crad in any way, but they could hear his deep voice talking and talking and talking, and after some time the Crad was saying meekly,

'Yes, sir. Certainly, sir. My mistake, sir. Certainly won't happen again, sir. Good evening, sir.'

And soon he flapped dustily off in his ungainly way. Every now and then he would look over his shoulder, his red eyes blazing, a heavy scowl on his face. Crark, Crark, they heard. But there was nothing he could do. And he soon disappeared into the dark.

'Here you are, young Bottle Rabbit,' Sam said, with a big smile and a little shake of his great head. 'And *please* try to be a more sensible animal.'

'Sam, I really didn't mean to. I'm really sorry. It was a sort of accident. I mean . . .'

But the Rabbit caught Emily's eye and with a sheepish grin tucked the Bottle back in his pocket.

12

'I'll really never do it again, Sam,' he said.

It was getting late. Emily and the Baker and the Rabbit all climbed on to Sam's broad shoulders. The Golden Eagle, who didn't like being on the ground for long, said, 'Bye,' and flew off fast to a meeting with some Arctic birds. And Sam set off across country towards Fred and Charlie's warm cabin. It was both cosy and exciting crouching up there in the dark, for it was night-time now and Sam covered the ground at enormous speed.

Fred and Charlie, who had been anxious all afternoon and evening, met them with happy smiles. 'Welcome home,' said Fred, and it hardly seemed any time before they were all sitting round a roaring fire, laughing and singing. Charlie had cooked a lot of sausages and had made a pie, and they ate these and drank hot drinks, sitting together round the fire and talking over the day's doings.

Emily was beginning to feel sleepy.

'How did you *ever* get the Bottle, Bottle Rabbit?' she asked sleepily, yawning and wrapping her tail round her front paws. 'And what can you really do with it?'

'Well, I got it as a Kindness Prize quite a long time ago. There was this old woman. I'll tell you all about it, but I think I'll have to tell you all that another time.'

He was right, because looking around he saw that Fred was asleep, and Charlie was asleep, Sam was asleep, the Golden Baker was asleep, and Emily herself was purring in the sleepiest way. So he folded his paws and settled down comfortably for the night.

2

The Magic Bottle

Emily usually slipped away during the night, in that mysterious competent cat way of hers, back to her own beech-tree home. But the night of the Crad business she felt she wanted to stay. Next morning she was up fairly early and found Fred pottering about in the kitchen. He was stirring a huge black iron pot of porridge over the fire and gulping down tea from an enormous china mug with roses on it.

'Hello,' he said, 'Charlie's outside, polishing up the cart and weeding the cabbages. What gets you up so early?'

'I know it's early, Fred, but there's something I'd like to ask you about the Bottle Rabbit, if it's all right. *He'll* never tell me – keeps saying he will but never does. Where *did* he get that magic Bottle of his?'

Fred took a big swig of tea.

'Let me finish my breakfast first, then of course I'll tell you.'

Finishing breakfast took a good long time. Fred had a bowl of porridge with cream and brown sugar. He then fried up some thick slices of smoked bacon, three eggs and a couple of fat sausages, some black pudding and some white pudding, cut some slices of bread and fried them too, threw in some mushrooms and sliced tomatoes, made another big mug of tea, then ate and drank the whole thing slowly and happily. Emily had the sense not to pester him with talk during all this. She did a little pottering herself, made some elegant thin slices of toast, deftly buttering them in her long delicate white paws, and had a breakfast-cup of coffee and milk.

At last Fred had finished. He bit down a couple of lemons to round off his breakfast, lit one of his curvy old pipes and, a little damp-eyed from the bitter fruit, began his story.

It all started (he said) one wet and windy day in March. The Bottle Rabbit (he was really just plain Rabbit in those days, but let's call him the Bottle Rabbit for convenience) was out in the woods tramping about. You know how he loves to do that.

He was quite a young inexperienced Rabbit then (not that he's exactly an old experienced Rabbit now, though he comes from a good background and has several well-respected friends, including me, I might add) and he had not really been about much.

In the woods it was raining terribly hard. The Bottle Rabbit sat down on a stone next to a roaring stream. It had been raining for two weeks without stopping, and the stream was in flood, so much so that the nearby stepping-stones were barely visible.

There did not seem to be anybody about. In fact the woods seemed strangely empty, as though everybody had deliberately run away, perhaps frightened by something or somebody. The Bottle Rabbit was quietly squeezing rain-water out of his paws when he suddenly noticed that he was not alone. An odd little old woman dressed in black, with a high conical black hat, was standing quite close to him at the water's edge, muttering to herself. She had a thin pointed nose, and a broad pointed chin. It was a very long nose and a very long chin. She had fierce black eyes and a withered neck, and she was carrying what looked like a broomstick. Toads hopped nearby on the cold stones, and all around was the whirring of small hairy creatures with red mouths and long tails.

Lightning flashed and thunder roared. The old woman's craggy face was lit with a greenish light in a great gap-toothed grin. She chuckled in a secret black and midnight way.

'What a hurly-burly,' she croaked, and then screamed with laughter.

'Yes,' said the Bottle Rabbit politely, 'it's certainly coming down hard, and the forecast only said drizzle. It's a bit weird here, too, when it's so dark.'

'*Weird*?' snapped the old woman sharply. 'I don't see anything *weird* about it. Nothing's *weird*.' She twisted and turned on her stone, and spiders and small land-crabs went running round and round it.

'But I do wish someone would help me over this stream. I'm wet through and it's not safe. I've got this heavy iron cauldron to carry home, and all kinds of groceries, too.' She rubbed her skinny hands together and cackled. 'Yes, all kinds . . . hope I haven't forgotten anything.' She was muttering to herself again. The Bottle Rabbit could not hear very well over the thunder, but she seemed to be counting things off on her twiggy fingers: 'newt . . . frog . . . wool of bat . . . smallage . . . wolf's bane . . . slips of yew . . . baboon's blood for the cooling . . . and I need more bones . . . more bones . . . more bones.' She writhed about.

17

'Er, if you want to cross the stream I'd be glad to help you, madam,' said the Bottle Rabbit cheerfully. He could see that she was old and frail. 'Just give me the big cauldron and take my arm, and we can still use those stepping-stones over the stream.'

The old woman stared at him, her eyes flashing red under her big-rimmed conical hat. Then, 'All right, young Rabbit,' she cried, 'help me you shall.' There came a great deafening screech of laughter. When the old woman laughed like that, the tip of her nose nearly met the tip of her chin. At the sound toads hopped about, a brindled cat mewed, more lightning flashed, more thunder roared. The ground around her looked slimy.

'Take my cauldron.' She handed it over. It *was* heavy. Soft things thumped and flopped about in it. 'And take my arm.' Another screech of laughter. She grabbed his plump woolly front paw with a skinny brown hand. Then came a yet louder screech of eldritch laughter. Forked lightning crackled.

The Bottle Rabbit could not see what was so funny, but he concentrated on getting the old woman to put her feet (*they* looked a bit funny, mind you, more like hooves, though he tried not to stare at them) on the middle of each stepping-stone. Surprisingly they were soon at the other side and safe on land.

The old woman panted and sat down on another stone beside the roaring flood.

'Well, I think I'll be pushing off now,' said the Bottle Rabbit.

'Nay, nay, tarry a while,' said the old woman.

'What?'

'Don't *go*,' she snapped, rather impatiently. 'I've got something for you. Who'd have thought it? A Kind

18

Animal after all. I'd never have believed it after this morning's caper. Look at me. Wet through. Stood there for an hour and not one single animal offered to lift a paw to help me. That fox. You might have thought I was the Devil or something, the way he took off; then there was the porcupine, turned upside down trying to get away. Scared stiff *he* looked. And three or four domestics, dogs, cats, a tortoise. A cow, too. Just as bad as the others.' Her face worked angrily.

'Anyway, this is getting boring. Here's your thing.' She felt about in her large crumpled leather bag. The old woman seemed to be moving bones and live things about, a thin black snake, a fat frog, his neck heaving, and a brown-and-green rat almost a foot long. 'Yes. Here we are. Here's your Kindness Prize, Rabbit. It'll fit in your right-hand pocket.' Her long skinny hand was holding out a smallish dark-green dusty bottle with a cork in it; used-looking.

'Oh. Thank you very much. You shouldn't have bothered,' the Bottle Rabbit stammered, a little puzzled. He took the bottle, looked at it, turned it over, then, rather embarrassedly, with a meek look at the old woman, took the cork out and peered in. It was quite empty.

'Er, thank you very much. It's a useful-looking bottle; it'll be useful.'

'Pongling's the thing – just remember that,' the old woman grinned. 'Pongling. Try it on your own. Pongle twice, pongle once. Goodbye.'

She stood up rather stiffly. 'And watch out for enemies. That Bottle is known to many bad souls. They'll try to buy it or steal it or find it somehow. Mark my words,' her voice rose to a screech again, 'only use it when you have to. Except when you want a bit of fun.'

'Fun?' said the Bottle Rabbit.

'Yes,' she screeched, 'one pongle, two pongles, like I say. Just open the bottle, shake, say "pongle" good and loud.'

She jumped on her broomstick, clapped her hands and hurtled off into the clouds. The Bottle Rabbit looked around. All the odd little crawling creatures had disappeared. He looked up into the sky, now clearing. All he could see was a tiny dot in the distance. A faint echo of her screeching laugh lingered in the air.

'Never seen that done before,' said the Bottle Rabbit to himself, shaking his big black ears.

Now, as I've said, he was an inexperienced young harmless rabbit, but he had a healthy touch of natural curiosity in him and had soon got the Bottle out again. He noticed for the first time that round the bottom rim there were tiny carved letters. They said:

> This truth ever bear in mind
> I'm only useful to the Kind.

'Hm,' he said, 'hope *I'm* kind. Now what was it she said? Pongle twice, pongle once? Well, might as well give it a try.'

It had stopped raining. The sun was rising calm and bright, and all the air was filled with pleasant noise of waters. He sat down on a dry rock under a spreading chestnut tree. Out came the cork, one shake, and

'Pongle,' he said. 'Pongle.'

Nothing happened. He sat there feeling a bit put out. She certainly had been a weird old woman. Yes, he'd said weird and he'd meant weird. He felt fed up.

Then came a little *plop*, and just at his feet lay a neat little package, a white freshly-laundered linen napkin folded round a sandwich of white bread with thick juicy ham, lettuce, and a little pot of hot mustard and a small silver knife.

'Golly,' he said, 'I'm going to try it again. Pongle, pongle.' And after a pause the same thing happened again. No knife this time, and the sandwich was chicken-breast, with home-made mayonnaise in a little pot, but it was just as delicious.

'Now I'll try one pongle.'

'Pongle.'

Another short pause, then – *plop* – and a large bottle of ice-cold lemonade was lying next to the sandwiches.

The Bottle Rabbit set to and made an excellent lunch. But as he was brushing the crumbs off his woolly back paws with one of the napkins, and thinking 'Not bad', he heard a sort of whistling grunt and looked up.

A white, fattish but quite good-looking pig, with a

toothbrush moustache, a small green pork-pie hat and a belted raincoat, was eyeing him.

'Nice bit of weather, old man,' said the pig.

'You mean it's stopped raining?'

'You're dead right. But nice storm too. Exciting. Reckon your Old Lady friend liked it too, old man. All that thunder and lightning. What do *you* think?'

'Old Lady?' said the Bottle Rabbit.

'Yes, that skinny old thing that fancies you. Gave you that funny old green bottle there.' The pig's little eyes swivelled towards it. 'Mind if I take a look at it, old man? I'm by way of being a bit of a collector of odds and ends of rubbish like that. For the colours, and the shapes, you know. Tell you what, old man, I'll take it off your hands if you like. I'm Ken, by the by; everybody calls me Ken.'

The pig seemed to talk faster and faster as he went on, and breathed more and more heavily. His little curled tail twiddled and twitched. He put out a trotter. (Ken was wearing kid gloves.)

'Well ... I ...' the Bottle Rabbit hesitated. He wasn't too keen on letting Ken take his Magic Bottle, even for a moment.

'Come on. Show it to us. What's the problem?' Ken pushed and shoved the Bottle Rabbit about a bit with his big white body, trying to get at the Bottle. Nothing rough, just shoving. The Bottle Rabbit slipped the Bottle into his pocket and gripped it very tight. He remembered the old woman's warning. Still, he didn't want to be rude, so he said:

'Well, if you just want to *look* at it, Ken, there's nothing wrong with that, I suppose. It's just a smallish

Bottle.' And he took it out and held it up. Ken immediately plunged forward and seemed to trip over by
accident and grabbed at the Bottle Rabbit to steady
himself. When Ken straightened up, *he* was holding
the Bottle.

'Funny little bit of a thing, isn't it, old man? Not
much use to anybody, I'd say. How much you want
for it? Five bob? Ten bob?'

'It's not for sale,' cried the Bottle Rabbit. 'Give it
back. It's mine.'

23

'Now then, temper, temper,' said Ken, smiling in a fat sort of way and waving the Bottle about in front of the poor Rabbit's worried face.

The Bottle Rabbit was *really* worried. Ken was much bigger than he was, and he couldn't think what to do next. Ken's grin got fatter and fatter.

It was just then that an enormous bear, an *immense* bear, came ambling up along the stream's bank. The bear was out for a stroll after all the rain, and he nodded in a pleasant, friendly way to rabbit and pig as he passed by. At first it seemed that he would just go walking on through the treeshade of sunnywinking leaves, smiling benignly. Then the bear looked again and saw the deep sorrow on the Bottle Rabbit's face.

'Hello. Something up, young 'un? Am I mistaken, or are you miserable about something or other on this beautiful sunny day?' His big shrewd bear eyes shifted to Ken, who had stopped grinning and was beginning to look uncomfortable.

'Well . . . sir . . .' began the Bottle Rabbit, nervously.

'Call me Sam,' said the bear kindly, for that was who it was, Sam the Bear.

'Oh, thank you, sir, I mean, Sam. He . . . he won't give me back my Bottle. And it's my own. It's mine. Somebody gave it to me.'

'Oh, he won't, won't he? Well, we'll soon see about that –' began Sam. But Ken, who had now turned a deep, dark red, laughed in an awkward hollow way:

'Ha ha ha ha *ha*. Nobody enjoys a good joke more than myself. You got me all wrong, old man. Just a bit of a misunderstanding. Just a bit of fun. I was just holding it up to the *light*, old man, holding it up to . . . I was just . . . I was going to . . . I . . .' Ken faltered and his voice trailed off. Sam the Bear was holding out a huge paw and staring at him in a firm manner.

Ken meekly placed the Bottle in that vast paw, shrugged his shoulders, turned and trotted off into the woods. He did not look happy, but he still managed a jaunty 'Have a nice day, folks. Goodbye, old man, and keep fit.'

'Let's have no more bullying of that kind in these woods,' Sam the Bear's great deep voice called after him.

'Right, old man. Quite right. Take care,' called Ken as he disappeared into the trees. He clearly cheered up pretty quickly, because in a minute they heard first a little piping whistle and then Ken's voice raised in song, in what must have been some foreign language. Translated, the song went roughly:

> Pigs, pigs, wonderful pigs,
> Known throughout the forest
> As the nicest and handsomest animals
> To be found in all creation
> And much beloved.

Sam the Bear smiled and shook his great head.

'He's not such a bad sort really, you know. I like a pig myself. Resourceful chaps. But that fellow just over-stepped the mark. Went a bit too far. Now show me where you live, young fellow, and I'll stroll you home.'

They ambled home together, talking twenty to the dozen about everything under the sun. They stopped once for the Bottle Rabbit to pongle up some lunch with his amazing Bottle, sandwiches and drinks, a first lunch for the bear, a second lunch for the rabbit. By the time they were back here they had become, as you know, extremely good friends, with much in common.

And of course we've all come to know, love and respect Sam the Bear.

'So *that's* how it all began. Thank you, Fred,' said Emily.

'Any time,' said Fred, puffing on his pipe.

'One thing, though. Who was that weird old woman?'

'Don't know any more than you do.'

'Perhaps we aren't meant to know?'

The horse gravely nodded his head and puffed quietly away at his pipe.

'And what else can the Magic Bottle do?' asked Emily.

'Perhaps you'll find out for yourself if you see enough of the Bottle Rabbit.'

'That's what I'm hoping to do,' said Emily.

At that moment the Bottle Rabbit appeared, rubbing sleep from his eyes with both paws and yawning. 'Oh. Good. Porridge,' he said. He got himself a bowl of it and some cream, and as it was such a nice day he sat on a bench outside to eat it.

Emily slipped out to sit on the bench with him. The Bottle Rabbit looked up, wiped a fleck of cream off his left front paw, and said, 'You wanted to know about how I got my Magic Bottle, Emily? Well, it was like this. I met this really nice old woman in the woods. It was pouring down, raining cats and dogs . . .' And he told her all over again, in his friendly Bottle-Rabbity way.

3

Bottle Rabbit and Poet

One hot afternoon, after another of their big picnics, Emily and the Bottle Rabbit left Fred and Charlie, napping with their pipes and little beer-barrels, and struck out into the deep, cool forest: a forest so deep and with trees so tall that at times you couldn't see the sun or even the sky at all. It was very quiet, too, as they walked along paw in paw. No birds sang, and the

only sounds to be heard were the cracklings of dried leaves and bracken underfoot. Emily often bounded ahead, a pale white graceful figure in the forest gloom.

The silent forest was almost too quiet. And soon, although neither animal said anything, they were both beginning to feel uneasy. So it was relief when a cheerful noise broke on their four ears, the splashing of water.

'Must be a stream.'

'Or a river.'

It *was* a river. They ran towards it and found themselves out in the open again. The sun shone brightly and the sky was blue. Better still, there was a good little sandy beach to lie on. Quickly they decided to bathe; and pretty soon cat and rabbit were kicking and splashing in the cool stream.

'I wish we had a ball or something,' shouted the Bottle Rabbit.

'There you go again. Never satisfied,' laughed Emily.

So he splashed her some more and they both laughed a lot and finally lay down in the sand to get dry.

Time passed. Then:

'Well, it's about time to be getting back.'

'Yes.'

'So let's start, shall we?'

'Yes, let's.'

They turned back towards the huge dark woods.

'Emily.'

'Yes?'

'Which way is it?'

'I . . . I don't know, Bottle Rabbit.'

'No more do I.'

They looked at each other worriedly. The truth is they were hopelessly lost.

'I know,' said Emily, 'we'll follow the river. Rivers always get *some*where.'

So they followed the river, sometimes finding stretches of walkable bank, sometimes leaping from stone to stone, sometimes clambering over rocks and fallen trees. They followed it and followed it. But it didn't seem to be getting anywhere.

'We're loster than ever,' said the Bottle Rabbit at last. 'But look, here's quite a big field. Let's sit down and think.' Both animals lay down in the grass and rested their weary paws.

'What am I *thinking* off?' cried the Bottle Rabbit suddenly. 'This is an open field. I'll get the six Blue Hares to fly in. Nothing could be simpler.'

'Six Blue whats?' asked Emily.

'Hares – *you* know – the quick-scuts, the grass-bounders. Four pongles on my Magic Bottle and they'll fly straight in and have us home in a brace of shakes.'

Emily watched interestedly as the Bottle Rabbit reached for his Bottle.

There was a gasp, and a stricken silence.

'Emily, the Bottle's gone.'

And it was true. His bottle-pocket hung open and empty.

'Oh my goodness. Oh my goodness. Where can it be? Where can it possibly be?' moaned the poor Rabbit. And Emily looked really pale and bothered now. How were they going to get back home to Fred and Charlie?

Then came a bizarre interruption. A chunky-looking goat in a business suit and with large boots on, carrying a bulgy briefcase, came trotting across the field towards them.

'Oh sir, thank goodness you've come,' cried the Bottle Rabbit. 'We are lost. Where are we?'

'Haven't the slightest idea,' said the goat. 'But I'm a poet, you see.'

'But we want to get home. Can't you help us?' said Emily.

'Not in that way. But I'll tell you what I *can* do.'

'What's that?'

'I'll read you one of my poems,' he said, first pulling at his beard, then groping in his briefcase. It seemed only polite to listen, so the Bottle Rabbit and Emily sat down on the ground at his feet. The poet looked at them for moment, cleared his throat and, standing with large boots pointing outwards, he began:

> A simple bleat
> Emerged from the neat
> Young lamb
> That stood at my side.
> And then came a rumble
> A mumble
> A grumble
> A stumble
> A cough –
> And it died.

There was a short silence. 'I call it "Lamentation",' said the poet, after a pause. 'Lamb – Lamentation – you get the idea?'

Emily looked unhappy, and the Bottle Rabbit, who was particularly fond of sheep, had tears in his eyes.

'What's *emerged*?' he whispered to Emily.

'Sort of *came out*,' she whispered back.

'You like "emerged"?' said the quick-eared poet. 'Yes, "emerged". It has its points. But I rather think "escaped" catches the elegiac tone better. Yes, "escaped" ' And he scribbled with a pencil on his poem.

> A simple bleat
> Escaped from the neat . . .

'Yes. I think so. I *think* so.'

'The cough and tumble part is very sad,' said the Bottle Rabbit timidly.

'Stumble, stumble. A stumble, a cough. You are right, however. Very right. It *is* a sad poem. But what I say is, if you put the unhappiness in the poem you keep it out of the life. You grasp my point? And it's the same with stories, by the way,' he said.

'Have you *any* happy poems?' asked Emily.

'Well, yes, indeed I have. Here's a very joyous one. It's called "There was a young man who said slag". It's quite short and I can repeat it by heart.'

'Oh *good*,' cried the Bottle Rabbit.

The poet folded his front boots, lifted his bony head so that he was staring at the sky, closed his eyes, and began:

There was a young man who said slag
Should be kept in some large leather bag.
This bag may be green
Or ultramarine
So long as there's plenty of slag.

33

'What's slag?' whispered the Bottle Rabbit.

'Industrial waste. From iron foundries,' whispered Emily.'

The poet was rummaging in his briefcase again. It had iron clasps.

'I've found another happy poem here; rather a longer one –'

'Actually it's getting rather late –' began both animals.

'It's a water poem. Happens at the seaside. It's a story. It's got a big creature called the Bulge in it, and Mr Groob and Agatha. You'll like it,' said the poet. He looked round gloomily and began again, waving his left front boot in time with his reading.

The Bulge, Mr Groob and Miss Agatha Flay
Sailed off in a boat on the rumbling sea.
With a flag on the prow and a rudder behind
They sat in the bottom and waited for wind.

The Bulge sat in front in a masterful way
With his feet on Old Groob, and his eyes on Miss Flay.
Mr Groob was, though somnolent, watchful and grim.
(You never knew quite what to think about him.)

Miss Flay, in the stern, in a beautiful gown,
Sat and stared at the water and thought with a frown:
'The Bulge, Mr Groob – what a curious pair.'
And sometimes she thought of her own glossy hair.

Nothing much happened, they just sat about,
Till at last the Bulge uttered a bellowing shout,
'Land ahoy! Goodbye, Groob, and farewell, dear
Miss Flay,'
And clambering up he dropped into the bay.

His enormous bulk darkened the waves as he sank.
Old Groob moaned, 'That's better.' Miss Flay just
looked blank.
The wind was now chilly, the water was cold,
Miss Flay shivered and shivered, and Old Groob
felt old.

They drifted to shore and sat down on a spar,
And Agatha got out some buns from a jar.
She said, 'Let's eat these.' Groob sighed, 'Yes, let's
indulge.'
And nobody thought any more about Bulge.

The End

'Well, I do like poems with lots of things happening,' said the Bottle Rabbit, hoping this was the
right kind of thing to say. The poet didn't answer, just
went on moodily swinging his boot.

'How did you come to *be* a poet?' asked Emily
brightly.

'Well, I should have been a rag-and-bone man, like
my father, and his father before him. They wheeled
their wheelbarrows through the broad and narrow
streets year after year. Famous, they were. But then
there wasn't the demand, so I took up poetry.'

'What's a rag-and-bone man?' whispered the Bottle
Rabbit.

'Mind you, what my father and grandfather used to
shout, up and down the back streets,' said the poet
with a hoarse sigh, 'that was the greatest poem I ever
heard, ever.'

'What did they shout?' asked Emily.

The poet straightened up, bent over with his front
boots out as though he were pushing a barrow, and

plodded slowly about. Then in a strange, wailing, crooning voice he called out:

'Rag Bo-o-o-one
Rag Bo-o-o-one
Any old jamjars
Any old jamjars
Rag Bo-o-o-one.'

The animals sat quietly.

'Let's push,' muttered the Bottle Rabbit.

'Well,' said Emily very loudly, 'we've got to get on our way now. It's really getting quite late. Thank you very much.' But how are we going to get back, she wondered, and suddenly, frightenedly, remembered that they were lost.

The poet was rummaging in his briefcase yet again and pulling out page after page. 'Here's another good one. A bit long, but some of it's happy. It's the story of –'

'YES, IT'S TERRIBLY LATE NOW,' yelled the Bottle Rabbit desperately.

''Mm. Yes. Here I have it. Yes, this is a trifle longer.' He held them with his glittering eye. 'There was a ship. I mean, it is the story, told in varying verse forms, of an ageing warrior rabbit who, after fighting long and bravely in the siege of a great city, is now journeying home with his companions to his faithful wife. He has many adventures, but I take up my story as this resourceful old animal, who has been washed ashore in a storm and lies sleeping near the beach, is approached by a beautiful young princess' (here Emily nudged the Bottle Rabbit) 'who, is, er, carrying some laundry. She speaks.'

Who can this old Rabbit be?
You Ocean waves O tell it me.

The Bottle Rabbit gave a sudden squeak. 'Did you say beach, *beach*?' he cried, slapping his black woolly thigh. 'Yes, yes, of course, what a fool I've been, what a complete fool. Wait here, Emily. Don't go away,' and he scampered off. The poet did not pause in his reading, simply went droning on.

The Rabbit was gone a long, long time, but just when the yawning Emily was beginning to give up all hope she heard a crashing in the undergrowth and out burst the Bottle Rabbit, who came bounding back across the field, hot, dusty, but laughing happily as he held up – his Magic Bottle!

The mighty Rabbit raised his powerful bow
And sent another suitor crashing low,'

chanted the poet, waving his head about without looking up. But Emily wasn't listening.

'Oh Bottle Rabbit. Thank goodness. Where was it?'

'I left it on the beach for safety when we went swimming. Then I forgot it,' he panted, and chuckled. 'Then *he* said beach, and I remembered. But let's get moving.'

He uncorked his precious Bottle and pongled four times – 'Pongle . . . Pongle . . . Pongle . . . Pongle.' And they waited.

As they sat waiting, the poet read on and on. It was a very long poem. He had just got to the last lines:

The well-pleased Rabbit now agreed to cease
And let the Goddess organize the peace . . .

when they heard a buzzing roar, and an elegant little blue-and-white aeroplane came swooping down to

37

make a perfect three-point landing in the field in front of them. The door flew open, a staircase unfolded, and six handsomely uniformed Blue Hares sprang out, lined up, and stood to attention:

'Yes sir.'

'Yes sir.'

'Yes sir.'

'Yes sir.'

'Yes sir.'

'Yes sir, where to sir?'

'Home,' said the Bottle Rabbit. 'Come on, Emily. Goodbye, my dear sir, and thank you for the verse.'

Emily was smiling happily. She too tried to say goodbye to the poet but he was already trotting away, looking calm, his hand on his heart, perhaps composing more poems. The Bottle Rabbit paused and turned as he was entering the aeroplane. 'Three cheers for the poet!' he called. The six Blue Hares raised their brightly plumed shakos and called:

'Hip, hip, Huzzah.
Hip, hip, Huzzah.
Hip, hop, Huzzah.'

and then in unison they sang, slowly and solemnly:

Ad multos annos, laude
Ad multos annos, laude
Ad multos annos gloriosque annos,
    laude, laude, laude.

The poet did not seem to notice. But Emily was pretty sure that she heard a faint 'Rag Bo-o-one, Rag Bo-o-one' in response as the door of the little plane closed smartly behind her.

While they flew home, one of the hares got out the card-table, put buns from a jar and lemonade on it, and the Bottle Rabbit, Emily and two of the hares played a cheerful round or two of Happy Families.

'What do they do with the rags?' asked the Bottle Rabbit, between deals.

'Make high-grade paper out of them,' said Emily.

'And the bones?'

'Glue.'

'What about the jam jars?'

'People put jam in them.'

Back home Fred and Charlie were waiting, as always, and as always were overjoyed to see them. Later that evening, as they were toasting a few final sausages at the fire and drinking cocoa before going to bed, Charlie pulled on his pipe and for once spoke. 'You know, Fred, it's a funny thing. I've always fancied being a poet myself.'

'Why don't you try doing some tomorrow morning, then?' said Fred, yawning. 'But it's bedtime now.' So they all went to sleep, warm and comfortable round the blazing fire.

39

4

Bottle Rabbit
Attacked by the Grumble

One fine spring morning the sun was shining bright and the leafy green woods were alive with light and shade; birds sang, bees hummed loudly in the glades and a beautiful young white cat came bounding gracefully along, her voice upraised in cheerful song.

> Spring, the sweet Spring
> Is the year's pleasant King,

sang Emily, for it was she, the Bottle Rabbit's friend.

> Then blooms each thing
> Then maids dance in a ring,
> Cold doth not sting, the pretty birds do sing . . .

Emily was swinging in one paw a little wicker basket with devilled eggs and a guacamole salad for two in it. She and the Bottle Rabbit were off for a picnic on their own, Fred and Charlie, their two Clydesdale horse-friends, both had work to do that day.

She had been up early devilling the eggs, mashing up the hard-boiled yolks, mixing in mustard, pimentos, red pepper, a touch of Indian chutney and just a dab of balsamic vinegar, finishing them off with a little sprinkling of caviare on top. She'd been careful with the guacamole as well, cutting an avocado in two, removing the stone, scooping out the flesh with a wooden spoon and mixing it up with fresh hot green chilli, a quarter of an onion, a tomato and some sprigs of fresh coriander. She was keeping it cool in a little earthenware pot. Her last act before hopping out of her hollow beech-tree house and closing its hidden door was to pop the avocado stone into a plant-pot, hoping to have a house plant from it some day.

Singing and bounding along, Emily soon came in sight of Fred and Charlie's cabin. The Bottle Rabbit was standing at the door waiting for her, looking very nice, his black furry body plump and polished, one white furry pocket bulging with the Magic Bottle. But there was something different about him.

'How do you like my new sunhat, Emily?' He was wearing a floppy white hat that perched between his ears and came down over his eyes.

'Well . . . er . . . it's very nice, very stylish.' To tell the truth, she thought it looked pretty silly.

They set off. The Bottle Rabbit was not carrying anything, no knapsack or small luncheon-hamper, for instance. Emily was a little surprised because he was supposed to bring half the picnic, by agreement, and after all, she had worked pretty hard that morning. But she decided not to say anything. She knew he had his methods.

The woods were so delightful in the spring sun that they walked a long way, up over a hill and down the other side, along a valley beside a splashy stream that gradually broadened into a river that led them to a large lake. The lake was so big, in fact, that they could only faintly see the far side of it. The place was beautiful, yet just a bit lonely and deserted-looking.

'You know, Emily, I think this must be Grumble Lake.'

'Grumble? What a funny name! Wait a minute, isn't there some story about it? No . . . there's something at

41

the back of my mind, though. But I can't quite remember . . .'

'Anyway, it's very beautiful, isn't it?' said the Bottle Rabbit. 'Let's have our picnic here.'

Emily spread a little table-cloth beside the lake and unpacked her devilled eggs and guacamole salad.

'Those look great, Emily. What's that stuff called?'

'Guacamole. Yes, I think you'll like it. It's Mexican, you know.' And then she couldn't hold back any longer. 'Er, Bottle Rabbit, what did *you* –?'

But the Bottle Rabbit was smiling and pulling out his Magic Bottle, withdrawing the cork and pongling twice: 'Pongle, Pongle.'

'Oh yes, of course!' said Emily. She had not actually seen this aspect of the Bottle before, and was wondering what would happen next, when – *plop* – in front of the Bottle Rabbit's paws appeared a sandwich of white bread, thick juicy ham and lettuce, all wrapped in a freshly-laundered white napkin, with a little pot of mustard and a small silver knife. He was pongling again twice: 'Pongle, Pongle.' And it happened again – *plop* – though this time it was a sandwich of tender breast of chicken on a bed of crisp, country-grown lettuce with farm-fresh home-made mayonnaise. Then the Bottle Rabbit pongled once: 'Pongle,' sat down, and – *plop* – a large ice-cold bottle of lemonade appeared.

Emily was entranced and the two animals settled down for a delightful picnic. For some time Emily told the Bottle Rabbit how she'd devilled the eggs and how she'd mixed the guacamole. Then they lay quietly, listening to the lake-water lapping with low sounds by the shore.

The Bottle Rabbit felt so happy that *he* decided to sing a song, too; it was that kind of cheerful spring day.

'Those waves remind me of the sea, and the sea reminds me of a good song. Listen to this, Emily,' and he sang away quite musically, glancing over at her every now and again:

> The Cat and the Bottle Rabbit sailed to sea
> In a beautiful dark-blue yacht.
> They took sausage and mash and plenty of cash
> Wrapped up in a five-pound . . .

'What?' asked Emily smiling. 'Wrapped up in a five-pound what?'

'I'm blessed if I remember. I've got some of the words wrong, I think. There's a whole lot more about a pig, and, yes, a turkey that lives on a hill. But I've forgotten most of the middle part. Anyway, I know it ends up like this:

> And paw in paw
> Along the shore,
> They danced by the light of the moon.

'The moon,' hummed the Bottle Rabbit, 'the moon, they danced by the light of the moon.'

43

Emily leapt up. The Bottle Rabbit took her delicate white paw in his furry one, and they danced and pranced along the lakeside under the shining sun.

Then came a loud roar, and a quite horrible, menacing Thing rose up in front of them. Not easy to describe: big, wet, shapeless and lumpy with bedraggled fur, gleaming yellow eyes like headlamps, and bare knobbly knees. On the back of one knee clung a tiny, spidery little creature with a bulging forehead and a scratchy voice.

'I'm the Grumble,' roared the monster.

'And I'm the Merritt,' squawked the nasty-looking

44

little creature, peering round the Grumble's huge bare knee.

'I'm taking you lot down to my den under the lake,' bellowed the Grumble.

'That's right, Grumble,' squawked the Merritt, 'take 'em down, make a good supper off of 'em, why don't you.' The Merritt sniggered. 'I expect your Mother would like a slice or two off of that one tonight,' he added, pointing a thin yellow finger at the astonished Bottle Rabbit. The Merritt's thin lips were wet, his eyes excited. As he spoke, his little moustache waggled and his legs moved spasmodically. What's more, although his fingernails were black with dirt he chewed and chewed on them incessantly.

In an instant the frightened rabbit and cat were swept up in one big leathery hand to the Grumble's rather smelly bosom. Then came a mighty splashing crash. The frightful creature had actually plunged into the lake and was swimming furiously fast down and down, winnowing the waves with one great arm and with his two trunk-like legs. The Merritt still clung like a leech to the back of one of the Grumble's thrashing knees. They could hear faint muffled cries of 'Go to it, Grumble! Go to it! Dinner-time, Grumble!'

The Bottle Rabbit and Emily were not getting very wet because of the big leathery hand clutched around them. But they were miserable.

'I'm not having much fun any more,' said Emily.

'No more me, and you know what? My white floppy hat came off. I've lost it in the lake.'

Emily couldn't help thinking to herself, well, at least some good comes out of just about everything. But the Bottle Rabbit folded down his ears glumly, and wondered what was in store for them now.

45

With a great swishing of water the Grumble tore far away into the sickly light at the bottom of the lake, where slimy things crawled with slow legs. He stopped at last and suddenly lunged into what seemed to be a solid black rock. It was in fact a heavy door that swung back, and he blundered through and shoved it

46

shut. They were in his den. They could see the little pools of water that had flowed in with them draining gurgling away down small drain-holes near the rock-door, which was shut tight. They were in a half-lit echoing cave, almost completely dry, though they could hear the outside lake-water booming against the rocks.

The Grumble dumped them in a corner, and they crouched there, glancing warily around. It was an enormous, cavernous room, lit only by the great fire that glowed at one end, sending purple shadows flickering around. Its light served only to discover regions of shade, dark corners, dark nooks and crannies, though a row of polished cooking-pots and sharpened kitchen knives mirrored the flickering firelight on one wall. The Bottle Rabbit glanced at these uneasily. Not a restful or a peaceful place to be. Adding to the two friends' sense of unease was the raucous snoring that came from behind a heavy, dusty curtain. Someone or Something else was lying over there.

The Grumble stared in that direction. 'Humph. Mother's asleep again. Must have been at the port.' The Grumble stared impatiently round. 'Merritt, bring me my pipe and bring me my bowl. And I want my three fiddlers.'

'No fiddlers, Grumble. We haven't *got* any fiddlers.' The little creature gave him his pipe and bowl. 'But *I'll* sing you something if you like. What about a nice Old English song? I could do you "Deor". Remember "Deor"? All about weal and woe?'

'Ugh,' said the Grumble.

'Well, how about "The Wife's Lament?" ' persisted the Merritt, his voice sounding like a dry wheel grating on the axle-tree.

47

'*Please.*'

'Well, I'll do "Wyrta", that's a good one; it's all about plants that cure blisters,' and the Merritt began to sing, or rather drone, in a groaning voice:

Now these nine worts are potent
against the red poison, against the purple poison,
against the white poison, against the blue poison,
against the yellow poison, against the green poison,
against the dark poison, against the blue poison,
against worm-swelling, against water-swelling,
against thorn-swelling, against thistle-swelling,
against . . .

'Merritt!' shouted the Grumble.

'Yes?'

'Shut up.'

'But there's more of it, Grumble, some of it marked by humour and lightness of touch,' and he droned on:

Have the cattle and hold the cattle
And bring home the cattle, and . . .

'Merritt, I *said* shut up, and I *meant* shut up.'

'Oh, *all* right.'

At last the ugly little creature quieted down, though he still muttered to himself. The Bottle Rabbit thought he heard something like, 'Hic ana wat ea rinnende,' whatever that might mean.

The Grumble had been swigging away, filling and refilling his bowl with thick, dark rum, and those yellow eyes of his were looking bleary now. They flickered round his hall, and fell on the two worried animals. The Grumble laughed harshly and started mumbling.

'Yes, I think a nice stew would be just the thing, first a little nap and then . . .' He half nodded off but

48

started mumbling again, slowly, '. . . a nice stew, a nice, nice stew, with celery and pepper and garlic and onions and oregano and mace and one rabbit and garlic and thyme and rosemary and a mustard-seed and bring to a slow boil with mace and onions and more garlic and . . . add the rabbit . . .' The Grumble's massive head sagged and he nodded off boozily, snoring as loudly as his Mother.

As soon as he was fully asleep the ugly little Merritt sneaked round on his matchstick legs and, leaning over the Grumble's bowl, he gulped and gulped and gulped at the dark rum, looking over his shoulder between each gulp and quickly refilling the bowl when it was empty. Soon he was stumbling and scrambling about. Soon he, too, was half-asleep, but not before he had scowled over at Emily and the Bottle Rabbit and screeched in a rum-thickened voice, 'Lovely shtew. Marvellous appetizing shtew. Besht eating-club shtew.' The loathsome little creature sniggered again and fell asleep, his slack mouth open, thinly snoring.

Now the two animals did not want to be cooked in stews for the Grumble, his Mother, and the Merritt. It was a very unpleasant idea for both of them. The Bottle Rabbit was in immediate danger, and Emily feared that she would come next. For a while the situation had never seemed worse, but as usual they both tried to look on the bright side.

'Emily, at last everybody's snoring,' began the Bottle Rabbit, just as Emily started to say,

'Look, they're all asleep. Perhaps we could think of something to do.'

The trouble was that for some time neither of them could actually think of any way out of their terrible danger. There they were, trapped in a dungeon, down at the bottom of a lake. Even the Bottle Rabbit's Magic Bottle could hardly be expected to bring any helpful friends down to the bottom of a lake.

Yet things changed, as so often they do in life. The Grumble's Mother began to wake up. Not that that didn't become frightening in itself, when she came lunging out into the cave. What they saw was a colossal haystacky heap of a shapeless kind of Thing, greyish-brownish, with straws sticking out everywhere. Muttering and moaning to itself, it staggered out from behind that curtain and held out two vast arms. 'Port! Port! I need port,' groaned the Grumble's Mother, flailing about with her heavy arms. 'I want more port, and where are my spectacles? Give me my spectacles.'

These last words gave the Bottle Rabbit a brilliant idea. He had seen the firelight glistening on the spectacles, great pebble-glassed things, over in a corner. So he hopped across the Grumble's den, grabbed them and slipped them under a greasy blanket. Then – and this was his moment of glory and a very brave act – he coughed loudly and cleared his throat.

'Who's that? What do *you* want?' screeched the Grumble's Mother.

'Me? I'm just an inexperienced, tender young Rabbit.'

'Good. We were thinking about stew for tonight.'

'No, please listen, Mrs Grumble –'

'Don't call me Mrs Grumble. I'm Grumble's Dam.'

'Sorry. Listen, Mrs Dam –'

'Don't call me Mrs *Dam*. Oh well, what's the use? *Go* on then.'

'Listen,' went on the Rabbit earnestly, with his heart in his mouth but trying to sound important, 'I happen to be in the fortunate position of being able to inform you of the whereabouts of – in fact, we know where there's a big barrel of port hidden.'

'Barrel of port? Of *port?* Why didn't you say so in the first place? Then lead me to it, Rabbit. Get me to that port double-quick. I want port.'

The plan was beginning to work.

'Where's me specs?' screeched the Grumble's frightful old Mother. 'Who's hidden me specs? I can't see a thing without 'em.' (This is what the Bottle Rabbit had counted on.) 'It's that feckless Merritt again, isn't it, singing his stupid songs and poking his nose into other people's business. Where are they?' But the Merritt and the Grumble went on snoring heavily, drenched in rum.

'No need to worry about your glasses, madam,' said the Bottle Rabbit suavely (Emily was amazed at the coolness he was displaying). 'If you can just open this great rock-door, the port-barrel – and I may say it is an exceptionally large specimen of its kind – lies just without. Your son deposited it there this afternoon. If you can push this rock open, you can pick up your port at the entrance and drink it down to your heart's content.'

'Of *course* I can open the door, idiot. Come and lead me over to the rock. Can't see without me glasses. What are you waiting for?' she roared.

Now began the most difficult and dangerous part of all. The two young animals crept over to where she was wavering about, each took hold of one of her loathsome leathery arms – bigger, fatter, speckleder and generally smellier even than her son's – and slowly led and pushed her over to the door.

'Port! Port!' she cried. 'Easy now, darlings,' she muttered. 'Where's the door? Where's my port?'

'Here we are,' gasped the Bottle Rabbit at last. 'Can you really push this open?' He nudged Emily, who nudged back.

'Of *course* I can, you foolish Rabbit. Where's my port?' she bellowed. 'I want it now.' And with that she threw herself against the rock-door with a terrifying thud.

It swung wide open. Water rushed in. Grumble's Dam stumbled out blindly, and quick as a flash, cat and rabbit flung themselves past her and up into the lake, kicking and kicking and kicking, and – in no time at all – with great gasping sobs of relief they found themselves up on the surface, gazing at a lovely white open-faced moon, sailing calmly across the bare heavens.

Then they raced for the shore as fast as they could. Both were strong swimmers and they arrived there neck and neck. They dragged themselves on to the sand, panting and shivering. The water had grown very cold.

'G-got to, g-got to g-get m-moving,' gasped the soaked Bottle Rabbit, who was quivering in the cold night. 'H-hares c-can't l-land h-here. N-no r-room. M-must get the m-m-mice.' He reached in his pocket for his Magic Bottle. It was there, thank goodness, and he quickly pulled out the cork and pongled five times, his wet ears flopping about as he stuttered: 'P-pongle . . . P-pongle . . . P-pongle . . . P-pongle . . . P-pongle.'

After a remarkably brief pause, during which both animals scanned the water worriedly for any signs of Grumble activity, the cheerful jingle of bridles and reins could be heard, a little posthorn rang out dis-creetly, and up trotted eleven over-sized, powerful-looking white mice, pulling behind them a bouncing, finely-carved ivory state-carriage with spangling wheel-spokes flashing in the moonlight. A twelfth mouse in elegant livery, who had been standing up behind the coach, laid down his posthorn and ran to swing open the coach door.

'Big warm towels and blankets inside, sir, and some hot tea with a little something in it,' called this cheery mouse.

'G-good. H-home as f-fast as you can g-go, p-please, N-Nigel,' gasped the weary Bottle Rabbit. He and Emily bundled in, and in a moment were bouncing along on the soft red velvet carriage-seats, towelling themselves dry, sipping their hot drinks from a little thermos bottle, and watching the sinister lake recede fast behind them.

'That was brilliant, Bottle Rabbit,' said Emily after a while. 'You never cease to surprise me.'

'Oh, I don't know,' said the Bottle Rabbit, blinking modestly. 'It just came to me after I heard him mentioning that his mum liked port.'

'Saved us from the cooking-pot, that's certain,' said Emily, shuddering delicately. She sat quietly for a while. But she was clearly thinking something over. After some minutes she leant forward.

'Mind you, Bottle Rabbit,' she said, 'it did sound like an interesting recipe. I mean, I'd never have thought of putting mace in with oregano, but I liked the rosemary and mustard-seed idea. Of course he over-stressed the garlic, a common fault with inexperienced cooks, and the celery didn't seem *such* a great notion to me; it *does* tend to dominate everything else . . .' She glanced over at the Bottle Rabbit.

'Oh, I *am* sorry,' she said. 'I didn't mean . . .'

The Bottle Rabbit said nothing and looked rather pointedly out of the window. After all, the Grumble's recipe *had* called for one rabbit.

The coach rumbled on.

'Bottle Rabbit, I'm terribly sorry. You know how obsessed we cats get with *cuisine* . . .'

54

The Bottle Rabbit still said nothing. His feelings were evidently pretty badly hurt. Emily even began to wish she could get his floppy white hat back for him. But that was gone for ever.

So after a while she tried again.

'Bottle Rabbit, what was that lovely song you were singing just before the Grumble turned up?'

'What song? Oh, yes, that old thing,' said the Bottle Rabbit, looking pleased in spite of himself. 'You know, I still can't remember the middle part of that song, but I do remember the nice quiet sleepy ending.' He smiled at her forgivingly and began to sing quietly and sweetly in a soft rabbit's voice.

> So paw in paw
> Along the shore
> They danced by the light of the moon . . .

'The moon . . . the moon . . . they danced by the light of the moon,' sang Emily, and she reached out and took the Bottle Rabbit's furry little paw in her own.

By this time both animals were so sleepy they could not sing any more, and the gentle swaying of the carriage and the soft pitter-patter of the mice outside soon sent them off. When they got to Fred and Charlie's cabin they had to be lifted out of the twelve-mouse carriage by their two strong horse-friends and gently laid down beside the fire, where they went on breathing deeply and peacefully beneath the visiting moon.

5

Bottle Rabbit and Bugatti

Emily and the Bottle Rabbit had agreed that it was a perfect day for a brisk walk. The trees were in their autumn beauty and the woodland paths were dry, so the little cat and the rabbit set off paw in paw in the golden afternoon. The air was clean and crisp and the fallen leaves crackled as they walked.

Quite soon they came to a fine grove of great, rooted chestnut trees, horse-chestnut trees in fact. Many chestnuts were lying in the grass, some still in their knubbed green cases, others broken out, lying moist and plump and brilliantly brown.

'Conkers,' said the Bottle Rabbit. 'Conkers – let's gather some bagfuls for the small animals back home. They'll love them.'

'Good idea,' said Emily.

'I'll tell you what,' said the Bottle Rabbit. 'I'll just nip back to Fred and Charlie and get some picnic baskets and knapsacks and we can fill them up.'

It didn't take him long, and soon both animals were busily filling up the knapsacks and baskets.

'Why *do* they like them so much? I've forgotten,' said the Bottle Rabbit.

'It's "Conkers", you know, that game you play with horse-chestnuts. You each thread one on a piece of string and hit the other person's.'

'Of *course*. Now I remember,' cried the Bottle Rabbit, slapping his woolly thigh, 'and if you're not careful you get rapped on the paw. *I* remember. But what's the aim of the game exactly?'

'I'm not quite sure,' said Emily.

'Ahem ahem,' coughed someone in a little high nervous voice. 'Ahem ahem. Up here. Ahem.' They both looked up into a chestnut tree and saw a slim, precise-looking little rabbit high on a branch. Not a squirrel, a rabbit; though a much littler rabbit than the plump good-sized Bottle Rabbit.

'Ahem ahem.' Then he started counting in little short breathless gasps. 'One – two – seven – eight – three – nine – twenty-eight – sixteen – five.' He was

holding out one paw and counting these numbers off on his other little paw.

'What *are* you doing up there?' asked the Bottle Rabbit.

'Why, counting the conkers in your basket. Just come to me whenever you want anything counted. Counting is my special thing, you see,' said the little rabbit, hopping down from branch to branch as he spoke and landing beside them with a cheerful grin. 'It's useful to be high up for counting.'

'Well, I'm the Bottle Rabbit, and this is Emily. What's your name?'

'I'm Count Hubert. I count. Any time you want anything counted you can count on me.'

'We certainly shall,' said Emily and the Bottle Rabbit together, smiling at one another.

58

Count Hubert looked happy and hopped about beside them as they resumed gathering the conkers. Then Hubert coughed. 'Ahem. By the way,' he said, 'in Conkers you win when you break the other person's conker.'

'You're absolutely right, that's it,' said the Bottle Rabbit, and on they worked.

They had filled four large knapsacks when there came a loud honking and an extraordinary-looking open car drove up the narrow lane that ran behind the chestnut grove.

It was long, low, rakish and powerful-looking, painted a bright golden-yellow. The bonnet stretched more than half the length of the long car and had big leather straps over it. There was a fold-back canvas-and-leather roof like on an old-fashioned perambulator, and the silvery spokes on the wheels glistened in the sun. There was a spare wheel strapped flat on top of the boot. There was lots of shining brass. There were running-boards, and on the driver's side there were levers and things *outside* on the running-board. The driver had a big loud plaid cap pulled flat on his head. He had heavy curly moustaches, dark goggles, kid gloves, and a luxurious-looking fur coat that went down to his ankles.

Emily thought the driver looked handsome, and found the yellow car quite interesting, but the Bottle Rabbit and Count Hubert literally danced with excitement at the sight of it.

The car's rather weighty driver switched off the engine and leapt quite gracefully out of his machine.

'Hi there, folks. Like the old bus? Not bad, eh? And she goes great, too. Care for a spin? Feel free to come along. The treat's on me.'

59

'Yes please, yes please,' cried the Bottle Rabbit and Count Hubert as one rabbit, and they hopped right in and sat on the other front seat side by side. 'Coming, aren't you, Emily?' said the Bottle Rabbit. But Emily felt differently. 'Thank you so much for your most kind invitation, sir, but on reflection I think I should prefer to linger here in this calm chestnut grove and gather in more of these attractive conkers for our deserving little friends.' Something indefinably unsatisfactory had struck her about this driver-person and made her talk in this prim fashion. Also she wasn't all that keen about roaring through the woods in a throbbing, stinking motor on such a perfect autumn day. Moreover, when the driver climbed back into the car himself, Emily happened to glance at his feet. And although under his fur coat he was wearing long, elegant crocodile-leather boots, somehow those feet looked remarkably like pigs' trotters. A nameless fear struck her.

'*Bottle Rabbit*,' she quickly called, waving a frantic white paw. 'Wait, Bottle Rabbit, there's something you must know. I believe it's . . .' It was too late. Her soft voice was drowned in a powerful roar as the driver opened up the throttle and the car shot off. The beaming Bottle Rabbit and Count Hubert waved happily over their shoulders as Emily stood there aghast. 'I think it's Ken,' she whispered to herself. 'Yes, it's Ken.' Emily had never met that suspect pig – though of course she'd heard from Fred about how Ken had tried to take the Bottle away from the Bottle Rabbit on the very first day the good-natured Rabbit won it as a Kindness Prize (Sam the Bear had stopped him that time) – but there was something about the driver's voice, clothes, manner, and now above all his feet, that gave her pause. 'I won't be happy till I see them back here safe and sound,' she said to herself as she sat down and went on sorting conkers. 'Those whiskers, the goggles and cap may well be just a disguise!'

Meanwhile the animals were rumbling along through the woods in the great yellow car. The Bottle Rabbit and Count Hubert found the bright red seats quite hard, as it turned out, and there was plenty of rattling, but the Bottle Rabbit especially was delighted by the gleaming brass carriage-lamps, the running-board with all its gears and tackle and trim, the dozens of dials and switches on the dashboard, and above all the huge honking horn, a sort of trumpet that curled round and round, with a big black rubber sphere to squeeze fixed on to it.

'Go ahead and blow the horn if you want to, old man,' shouted the driver above the noise of the car's engine. 'Feel free to squeeze it. Be my guest. Give yourself a thrill.' He twirled his curly moustaches as the Bottle Rabbit happily squeezed on the rich horn and got a loudish honk out of it.

'Care to see a turn of speed?' yelled the driver. (The engine was extremely loud now.) The Bottle Rabbit and Count Hubert nodded excitedly. Then came much fiddling with dials, knobs and levers. 'Hold on to your hats,' cried the driver. 'But we haven't got any hats . . .' the Bottle Rabbit was beginning to say when, with a deafening clatter, the car surged forward and they zoomed away. In fact they were not really going very fast, but it feels fast when you are driving in a large car down a small country lane between lots of trees.

'Ain't this old girl a beauty?' bellowed the driver as they whizzed along the country lane, the trees flying over their heads. Then, as they began to slow down,

'Care to take the wheel, old boy?' The Bottle Rabbit could hardly believe his long floppy black ears. 'What? Me drive it?' 'Sure, why not?' 'But I've never ever even . . .' 'Apple sauce! It's as easy as pie. Here, I'll show you the whole bag of tricks.' The driver stopped the car and started showing the eager Rabbit what he had to do, pushing this and pulling that.

To the Bottle Rabbit's surprise it seemed fairly simple after all, just a few little movements. 'But what about all those switches and dials, and the levers on the running-board and stuff? Can't I use those too?'

'Oh. That comes later when you've had more experience, old boy. That's for your more refined driver. Your expert. See what I mean? Oh, and you can put this spare cap on.' He produced another large plaid cap.

Soon the Bottle Rabbit was bowling along with an enormous grin on his pleasant rabbit's face, with Count Hubert hopping about beside him and counting like a mad thing. The big cap was falling over the Bottle Rabbit's ears and eyes, and the car weaved about a bit, but they drove round and round in the woods for ten minutes or so until the driver said:

'OK. Let's take a break. Take five,' and he helped the Bottle Rabbit to stop the car. They all got out.

The driver flattened his cap still further over his ears and straightened his goggles.

'Well, what do you think? Like her, don't you?' He patted the bonnet.

'Like it? I love it,' said the Bottle Rabbit.

'It's pretty nice,' said Count Hubert.

'She's got two-way sprockets, you know,' said the driver, '*and* chamfered groining.'

'Oh, good,' said the Bottle Rabbit, 'and what are

those little holders for?' pointing to two little metal pockets on the inside of the doors.

'Flowers. Fresh *or* artificial. Nice if you're bringing a lady friend along.' The driver nudged him playfully. 'This is a 1932 Bugatti, you know. Says so on the front. An authentic antique automobile anyone would be proud to own. Imagine your family's squeals of delight when they see this beside the kerb outside your home. Your friends will look at you with a new respect. There's people'd sell their souls for a vehicle like this. Their souls.'

'I know,' said the Bottle Rabbit.

'I like you, you know,' the driver went on. 'You're what I'd call a real gentleman car-fancier. So I'll tell you what I'll do. How about making a deal? How about swapping my car for . . . Let's see. What've you got? Anything worthwhile?'

'Well, I've got my Magic Bottle,' said the Bottle Rabbit doubtfully, 'but you won't want my Bottle.'

'Oh, I don't know about that, old boy. I like bottles. I'm definitely interested. All my family's been interested in bottles for generations back.'

'Really?'

'Oh yes. It's in the family. In the blood. Tell you what, I'll make a sacrifice. I'll swap my car for your Bottle and I'll throw in that spare plaid cap, too. What say? Is it a deal?'

The Bottle Rabbit couldn't believe his good fortune. He felt he'd never ever wanted anything in all his life as he wanted this car. He began to explain to Count Hubert: 'You see, I won't need the Blue Hares or the mice any more when I've got this, will I?' Count Hubert, who knew nothing of the Magic Bottle and its powers, nodded obediently. He was busy counting

the spokes on the car's wheels. 'Ahem Ahem. Seven –
eleven – nine – two – forty-two – sixteen – eight.'

'And who needs sandwiches and stuff?' went on the
Bottle Rabbit. 'Anyway, I *love* the car. I really *want* this
wonderful car.' Count Hubert nodded, his lips moving
rapidly. Then, turning to the driver, the Bottle Rabbit
said, excitedly and rather indistinctly, 'Yeah.'

'Come again?' said the driver.

'Yes I said yes I will Yes.'

The driver immediately held out the car keys,
breathing heavily.

Then a thought struck the Bottle Rabbit and he hesitated for a moment. 'There's one thing,' he said earnestly. 'Are you kind? It's important.'

'Kind? Me Kind? Well, I don't know about that, old
chap, but I *can* say that down at the club there's not a
more popular figure than old Ken – er – old Denis, I
mean. That's my name, Denis, see? Only last week the
chaps gave me a presentation, as a matter of fact, a sort
of testimonial, don't you know, framed in light oak:
"To Denis from all of us at the Motor Club, in appreci-
ation". Did it off their own bat. Just like that. That tells
you something, doesn't it?' He twirled his huge
moustaches quickly and watched the Bottle Rabbit out
of the corner of his shrewd little eyes.

'Well, that's all right then,' said the Bottle Rabbit,
relieved. 'If you want to swap, I'll swap.'

'Done and done,' said Ken (for it *was* Ken, of
course). 'Here's the car keys and now, let's have the
old bottle, old boy. We'll stick it in the old collection.
Tickled pink my old dad'll be.' He watched anxiously
as the Bottle Rabbit pulled the Bottle out of his pocket;
then he grabbed it, stuck it in the pocket of his fur coat,
and was turning quickly away when,

'Oh, one last thing,' said the Bottle Rabbit.

'Well what?' said Ken snappishly.

'Where do you put in the stuff that makes it go?'

Ken showed him rapidly, then hurried off into the woods with the Magic Bottle. The Bottle Rabbit leapt back into the car and started it up in triumph.

So that was how, about seven minutes later, Emily, who was now curled up, taking a little rest, came to see the Bottle Rabbit wobbling up in the big yellow car, with a great happy smirk on his face.

'Jump in, Emily. How about a little spin? *Come* on.'

She still wasn't keen. She was bothered about the Bottle Rabbit driving, and she was also wondering where Ken had got to. But the Bottle Rabbit seemed so eager that she shrugged her shoulders and leapt in, and off they went – for about three-and-a-half minutes, that is, when KLONKK – KLONKK – KLONKK – KLONKK. Smoke – steam – nasty smells – and the Bugatti wobbled to a sudden dead halt. They all sat still in the smoking, steaming, dripping car and for a minute nobody spoke.

Oddly enough the car had stopped beside a little garage. In front of the garage was an old broken-down baker's van. Somebody was lying on his back under the van, fiddling about. After a while the Bottle Rabbit heaved a great sigh and honked his horn. It worked, and a middle-aged weasel in oily overalls slowly wriggled out from under the baker's van and strolled over.

'In trouble, eh?' he said, eyeing the car. 'What's this contraption then?'

'A 1932 Bugatti.'

'In a pig's eye it is. It's no more a Bugatti than I am.'

'Well, it says it is on the front,' said the Bottle Rabbit uneasily.

'I don't care what it says on the front. Let's have a look-see.' The weasel moved over and slowly opened the hood, bent over and looked inside at the engine for a minute, stuck a finger in one ear and twisted it round, then beckoned to the Bottle Rabbit.

'Hey, you in the cap,' he said, 'come over here and take a look at your famous Bugatti.' The Bottle Rabbit hopped out worriedly and stared under the bonnet, not quite sure what he was supposed to see or say. What he did see was mostly empty space and a tiny little engine that was smoking and bubbling. It didn't seem right, but he had no idea what all this meant and finally looked up at the weasel, who licked his lips. 'Leakin' oil,' said the weasel. 'Looks like a cracked cylinder-head to me. Gettin' *that* off'll be a job and a half in itself. Not to mention findin' the right gaskets.

66

You can't get 'em any more. Nobody wants 'em, see? And your big end's conked out too, I'd say.'

'Conkered out?' quavered the Bottle Rabbit.

'*Conked* out. Done for. No good. Same as your exhaust manifold. That's what's made all that roarin' noise. Hurts my ears, that roarin'. You can't get your parts, you know. Of course, you might pick up some odds and ends in a junkyard, but I doubt it. Nobody wants 'em, see?'

Count Hubert glanced at Emily and shrugged his shoulders dismally. The weasel's overalls said 'Frank's Body Shop' across the front.

'You mean you can't make it go?' groaned the Bottle Rabbit.

'Make it go? Well, if you lot all got out and shoved it you could get it under that tree over there out of everybody's way.'

'No, no. I meant make it go so that I can start the engine and drive it and everything.'

The weasel stared at him blankly, then shook his head in a slow, pleased way.

'Not this old heap of junk I can't. Beats me how you got this far. Where'd you find it, anyway? At the back of a barn?'

The Bottle Rabbit looked at him miserably.

'It's just a big heap of nothin',' went on the weasel, scratching himself under the arm. 'A lot of painted tin and bits of fancy brass and chrome stuck on top of a used-up little runabout from God knows where. Someone's been having you on.' The weasel laughed slowly and strolled away.

The Bottle Rabbit was shattered; he couldn't think or speak. His two friends stared at him in silence. 'Count Hubert,' said Emily suddenly, 'how did he come to be driving it?' And then a thought struck her. 'Oh, Bottle Rabbit, you can't possibly have exchanged –'

But the Bottle Rabbit was staggering away, clutching his head in his paws. Emily and Count Hubert picked up the knapsacks and baskets of conkers and glumly followed him over to a grassy knoll where they all flung themselves down. Emily reached for the Bottle Rabbit's paw, but he was too unhappy to be comforted. He'd lost his Magic Bottle in a useless exchange.

Then came a welcome interruption as a distant chanting broke the sad silence. They could hear it far away, far and clear, faintly blowing, high in the air. It came nearer and nearer and louder and louder; it was the sound of many, many voices, and now they could distinguish what was being sung:

We ARE the Boll-en-gers. We ARE wild ducks not farmyard ducks.

and again, now loudly and trenchantly, like the sound of horns and trumpets:

"We ARE the Bollengers. We ARE wild ducks not farmyard ducks,"
and a great flock of wild ducks came sweeping down towards them. 'Ahem ahem. Four – twenty-eight – eighteen – sixty-two – bother, I've lost count – eleven – four – and twenty,' Count Hubert was babbling away at high speed, trying to cope with it all. The brilliant birds landed all around them with a great whirr of wings. Their leader, a large handsome duck with green, dark blue and golden colouring and several rows of campaign medals across his chest, strode over and saluted the Bottle Rabbit. 'Good afternoon, sir, you may remember me. We met one evening last spring at a reception at the Golden Baker's. The Golden Eagle was also present, I recall. I remember we chatted with you at some length about sandwiches.'

Emily, never at a loss, was quick to greet the wild ducks in her gracious way. 'How pleasant to see you all. Do sit down. What a lot of you there are. How big in fact is your group?'

'We are nine-and-fifty, all counted.'

Count Hubert pricked up his ears at the word.

'That *is* a lot of ducks,' said Emily.

'Yes. We've found that in wild-ducking numbers count.'

Count Hubert looked at the Head Bollenger with great interest. He'd never heard of numbers actually counting before.

'And how are *you*, Bottle Rabbit?' asked the Head Bollenger, smiling at that poor animal.

The Bottle Rabbit was so miserable that he could hardly get a word out. But he was very polite always and did his best to greet these friends. 'Oh hello, hello there. Have you come far?' he stammered.

Now the Head Bollenger was no fool and quickly saw that something was wrong. He took Emily aside. 'Something up?' Emily explained how the Bottle Rabbit had been tricked into exchanging his wonderful Magic Bottle for a useless old fake Bugatti that didn't go. The Head Bollenger listened carefully and nodded a few times, his dark intelligent eyes darting here and there. His eyes lit on the knapsacks and baskets bulging with conkers. 'Mm-yes, mm-yes, I think so. Listen, Emily, that mountebank can't be far away. I think we wild ducks know how to deal with that old rascal Ken.' 'You mean you *know* him?' 'Oh yes. Everybody in the forest knows Ken. Now listen. Give me those knapsacks and baskets and follow us. Don't worry. Just look up into the sky and run over to where we stop and start our circling. Ken'll be there and he'll be getting a bit of a surprise.'

The Head Bollenger gave his flock, who were sitting at ease in a circle, a quick briefing. At a word from their leader the ducks seized the conkers and all suddenly mounted and began to scatter, wheeling in great broken rings. The Bottle Rabbit, Emily and Count Hubert, full of new hope, watched the splendid birds as they flew off and soon saw that they had regrouped and were circling over a spot quite close by. They raced over to it as fast as they could. None raced faster than the Bottle Rabbit, who hopped ahead of them, his eyes gleaming. In no time at all they found Ken standing in a little clearing with his fur coat open and looking distraught. He had taken off his big curly moustache. (Emily had been right, it *was* a disguise.) Now he was

shaking the Bottle in one trotter and pongling as if his heart would break. 'PONGLE, PONGLE, PONGLE,' he went, in big unhappy pig-pongles, and his real little toothbrush moustache jumped up and down. 'I *know* this is right,' he gasped irritatedly. 'I know it.' But nothing was happening.

Then down swept the magnificent Bollengers, armed with their conkers, and in a second they were raining on Ken. 'Ahem Ahem. One – nineteen – fifty-one – twenty-three – six – four hundred and thirty-two,' shouted Count Hubert in a vain attempt to keep up. Ken was trying to dodge conkers, hopping up and down like a herring on a griddle. 'Oh come off it, you ducks,' he yelled.

Now, for a rather portly pig to be pelted with conkers by nine-and-fifty determined wild ducks is no joke, and although Ken was trying to keep his aplomb he really didn't like it at all. The Bollengers were good-natured birds and none of them threw very hard; still, they knew what they were doing, and every now and again a conker caught Ken smartly on the nose, or slipped down his back. 'Ouch,' he cried, 'watch it. You nearly got me in the eye that time.' Pretty soon he had had enough.

'Oh, *all* right,' he said, 'have it your way. I give up. Just stop throwing those conkers, OK? Here, take your Bottle, Bottle Rabbit.' He handed, or rather trotted, it over to the delighted Rabbit. 'Satisfied now? Can't get the blasted thing to go, anyhow. Fat lot of use it's been to me.'

Immediately the wild ducks, who, like the Golden Eagle, never stayed very long anywhere, made one final swooping surge across the group of animals, let their last conkers drop harmlessly in the grass, then waved their companionable wings in farewell and flew away. As they disappeared into the distant skies the little group could hear their mysterious chant begin and repeat itself and fade far away, echoing and re-echoing:

> We *are* the Bollengers. We *are* wild ducks not farmyard ducks.
> We *are* the Bollengers. We *are* wild ducks not farmyard ducks.

Count Hubert, Emily, Ken and the Bottle Rabbit now stood staring at one another rather embarrassedly, though the latter still had a huge smile on his face as he grasped his recovered Bottle.

'Now I suppose *you*'ll say it's that Kindness business,' grumbled Ken at last. 'I don't think it's fair, you know. I really don't, old man. A trade's a trade. Fair's fair.' He shuffled about disgruntledly and pulled a couple of conkers out that had got stuck in the back of his fur coat.

'Oh come now, Ken,' said Emily. 'Don't tell us you weren't playing a pretty cheap trick on the Bottle Rabbit with that imitation Bugatti. *That* wasn't very kind.'

Ken gave a sheepish grin (unusual in a pig). 'Well, I suppose I *was* pushing things a bit,' he said. 'Still,' he brightened up considerably, 'it was a neat little job. Notice those headlamps? Could have fooled anybody. And what about that horn? Eh? Bet I could have unloaded that Bugatti on half-a-dozen other dumbos I know. Oh, pardon me, old boy, no offence meant. Just a manner of speaking.' He now grinned quite happily.

The Bottle Rabbit tried to look distant and offended, but he was smiling so much about having his Bottle back that he couldn't really manage it. 'No hard feelings then, old man?' said Ken quickly. 'No offence taken?' 'No. None. No offence in the world,' said the Bottle Rabbit. 'I'm so glad I've got back my Bottle. And I did like the car. And I hope the conkers didn't hurt much. There is one thing, though. Can I keep the spare motoring cap?'

'It's all yours,' said Ken tiredly. 'My pleasure. Be my guest.'

'Oh thanks,' said the Bottle Rabbit, and pulled the big bright plaid cap down over his eyes and ears.

Emily shuddered slightly, but said nothing.

'Certainly suits you fine,' said Ken. 'Well,' he shuffled about a bit, 'reckon I'll hit the road. See you, then.

Don't take any wooden nickels.' And away he trotted, a little crestfallen but with his head up and his trotters twinkling.

'Oh – sir,' squeaked Count Hubert.

'Yes?' Ken stopped.

'You forgot your moustache, sir. You dropped it.' And Count Hubert hopped over and handed the curly extravagance to the pig.

'Thanks a lot, kid. Thanks. And remember, keep up that counting. You could make a lot of money that way.' And Ken trotted jauntily off. He was still wearing his long fur coat, and in his own way looked rather striking with his kid gloves and long crocodile-leather boots. They could hear him whistling away and then his musical voice burst into one of his cheerful pig-brags. They couldn't distinguish the words of the song, but the ringing chorus went:

> More happy pigs
> More happy, happy pigs,
> Forever warm.

They decided to leave the conkers for another time. The Bottle Rabbit took out his bottle, removed the cork, and pongled up a few quick sandwiches to the amazement of Count Hubert, who had never seen the Bottle work. (They had ham, chicken, and a nice country pâté.) Then they set off home, taking the happy little rabbit with them. As they strolled back, 'Emily,' said the Bottle Rabbit, 'May I ask you a very special favour?'

'Of course.'

'Well, *don't* mention this afternoon's goings-on to Fred and Charlie, and especially not to Sam the Bear, tonight. I mean, I've been pretty silly again, haven't I?'

74

'Bottle Rabbit, it's bound to be all over the forest by now. But don't worry. They'll understand. After all, they're used to you being a bit of a . . . I mean, they know you sometimes get mixed up. They'll be nice about it, I promise you.' Emily looked at him. 'But there is one thing, Bottle Rabbit. It might be sensible not to wear that huge cap. It does rather draw attention.' He sighed and, to Emily's relief, took it off again and rolled it up in a paw.

And, of course, that evening everybody was terribly nice, though as they sat round the fire eating plaice and chips (with Count Hubert doing a little sleepy counting of the chips) Charlie did have a certain kind of look in his eye, the Bottle Rabbit thought, and Sam the Bear spoke at some length about a certain rascally pig variously named Basil or Denis or Ken, who had recently been called before the Council of Pighood and Decency for a reprimand, and Fred did bring up the topic of the lost joys of motoring for a while until Emily could get him back on to cooking. So the Bottle Rabbit was soon quite ready to doze off to sleep.

He still had a few thoughts to think, though. How could he possibly have . . .? he thought sleepily to himself, dozing off. What strange things we rabbits do. He smiled sleepily. Still, the car had looked rather splendid – those brass headlamps, the horn . . . He yawned. And Ken had been very nice to him really, and looked terrific, if a bit fat, in that fur coat and those crocodile boots . . . but now the Bottle Rabbit, with the Magic Bottle safely back in his pocket and his friends all around him, was ready to forget motor cars and pigs and boring weasels and to dream peacefully about distantly chanting Bollengers, and gondolas, and especially about hay-wagons ambling slowly down

75

deep warm country lanes, drawn by sleepy horses with battered old straw hats flopping over their great ears. So that's what he did. And Emily slept nearby, next to little Count Hubert and good old Fred and good old Charlie.

6

Bottle Rabbit at the Funfair

The little merry-go-round churned on, clanking and squeaking, and the steam-organ in the middle of it whistled and blared out hurdy-gurdy brass-band songs. All the winged elephants and swans and camels rose and sank, and the Bottle Rabbit and Emily the Cat and Count Hubert all clung close to the necks of their red-and-yellow-painted beasts and rose and sank with them. Little Count Hubert, as usual, was counting away, trying to calculate the number of people he'd passed as the merry-go-round turned and turned. 'Ahem Ahem. One – four – twenty-three – sixteen – nine – six hundred and one.' It was hard work for him, as they were moving at a considerable pace: the old stoat in the middle of the merry-go-round was winding the handle that kept it going with some vigour.

Nobody of course minded that Count Hubert was getting it all wrong, *mis*counting, in fact. Nobody ever did. Also, it was his birthday. Emily was laughing happily, but the Bottle Rabbit was not laughing at all: he was smiling politely, and he frequently waved a paw to Fred and Charlie, their two trustworthy Clydesdale cart-horse friends, who stood smoking their pipes and looking on. His black woolly body, however, was full of perturbation. Something was preying on his mind. All afternoon the Bottle Rabbit had been wondering whether he really wanted to go on the

big dipper, the towering roller-coaster that stood at the centre of the fair. Even as they bumpily circulated on this safe little merry-go-round with their small friend, the Bottle Rabbit could hear the big dipper's crash and rattle and swoosh, and also the distant screams of various daring animals as they climbed and swooped and dipped and swerved and rose again higher on that fearsome machine. Should he try it or shouldn't he?

This has been their fourth go round. So when the shirt-sleeved old stoat stopped turning his handle and the calliope gave a dying squawk and ceased tooting joy and hope, Fred called to the three animals to get off. As they scrambled down the little roundabout's battered wooden steps, Count Hubert asked if they could now go on the swings. But Fred had a better idea: 'Time for ice-cream,' he said, and Charlie, puffing blue smoke from his large curly pipe, nodded in agreement. The three of them had already been on the dodgems and the helter-skelter and had shied wooden balls at the coconuts and fired air-rifles at the ping-pong balls and rolled pennies down the little chutes and had seen the Hairy Man, the Iguana, the Gnu and the Fattest Woman in the World. So Fred winked and nodded at Emily and the Bottle Rabbit, who nodded back and now strolled off on their own for a bit to look round the fair. 'See you at the beer-tent in half an hour,' Fred called after them. As it turned out, that was not to be.

They wandered along over the well-trodden grass, past various noisy stalls, sometimes having to dodge exuberant animals who laughingly threw streamers or bounced little balls at them. The Bottle Rabbit kept edging towards the big dipper and edging away again. A lot of bears, of all ages, were aboard, out on a spree. The dipper did seem toweringly high. And the animals did scream all the time.

'What do you think, Emily?'

'No.'

'Sure?'

'Yes.'

'Well,' said the Bottle Rabbit, sounding relieved on the whole, 'what about that Voyage of Ghastly Ghosts thing?' He was looking over at a mysterious-looking booth. Outside it a big sleek-coated Labrador in a stiff white collar was barking about all its excitements and trying to sell tickets for it.

'Travel down the River of Fears,' he barked. 'See the Haunted House. Thrill to the ghastly sounds of distant times. Don't miss the Horror Room Hall of Darkness. Yes – the Voyage of Ghastly Ghosts – all for 50p!' The

Labrador barked and barked most enthusiastically and looked genuinely eager to get animals to come in and ride in his boats. The Bottle Rabbit was listening carefully.

'That thing's pretty scary too, you know,' he said to Emily, 'just about as scary as anything else in the funfair.' Another, louder scream echoed from the big dipper. He went on quickly: 'You go in a boat through all these strange dark scenes, and strange beings loom up and scare you. Let's try it while Count Hubert is having his ice-cream. After all, he's a bit young for this sort of stuff.'

'I'll tell you what, Bottle Rabbit,' said Emily, 'I think I'll wait for you outside. I'm not a big ghost-fancier myself.' Emily of course was a cat, and knew the real night scene and night mystery. She had done her share of prowling under a gibbous moon. 'So why don't you go and have a trip round by yourself, and tell me about it when it's over?'

The Bottle Rabbit agreed, braced himself, paid his pennies at the entrance, hopped into a large boat and set off, sitting all alone. The idea was that the boat moved by itself from one ghostly chamber to another and you sat there and were terrified. Wild screeches echoed through the halls and tunnels and every now and again bluish-greenish faces would loom up and disappear again. Bones rattled. Deep bells tolled. A sea-cow moaned and groaned. 'Just the usual sort of thing,' the Bottle Rabbit said to himself, keeping his ear on the dugong and averting his eyes from the bluish-greenish faces. 'Kids' stuff really. Meant to frighten you. It doesn't frighten me – much – really. Still, I wish Emily was here.'

Then all at once it got very, very dark and the boat

began to move past some bright bobbing grinning skulls. 'Not real, of course,' he said to himself. Then the Bottle Rabbit thought he caught a whiff of old breadcrumby waistcoats, and yes, of stale water in flower vases. And suddenly, in the thick dark, something leathery and nasty scraunched up against him in a suffocating way. Then a hoarse voice muttered horribly: 'All right. I'm in yer boat. Yerss. I'm in yer boat. Yer can't get away, yer know. I'm in yer boat. Just sit still in yer boat and go on havin' fun.' A hoarse cackle. 'But don't think of movin', mind. I wouldn't like that. Just sit still.' And claw-like hands, or hand-like claws, started tugging and scratching at the poor Bottle Rabbit's pockets.

'Ow!' he cried. 'Stop it.'

'Where is it?' croaked the voice. 'Don't move. I know it's 'ere. 'Ere it is.' The tugging and scratching continued. 'Yep, got it.'

'Ow,' cried the Bottle Rabbit again, and then he heard a suppressed 'Crark, Crark.' It couldn't be. But yes, it was. It must be. That voice, that stale breadcrumby smell . . . 'Can't see me now, can yer? Well, take a quick look so's yer can tell yer friends.' And a little light flicked on. None other than the Crad was holding a flashlight up under his own grinning face. 'Yerss. It's me all right,' the Crad croaked triumphantly. 'Followed yer in. When yer wasn't lookin'. When yer friends wasn't lookin', neither.' He cackled again in that dry way of his. The poor Bottle Rabbit sat hunched on his boat-bench. How hot and stuffy that haunted room – it was the Horror Room Hall of Darkness – felt now!

If the Crad had looked awful up in a tree in broad daylight last time they had met (he'd trickled the Bottle

Rabbit then into exchanging his Magic Bottle for a bag of gold that had turned out to be only withered brown leaves), imagine what he looked like now in the Horror Room with a small light shining up below his big jagged beak. From where the Bottle Rabbit was sitting it seemed that the Crad had a large mouth which was full of long teeth. These teeth were about one foot long and as thick as cow's horns. His body was almost covered with long black hair like a horse's tail hair. He was very dirty. And worst of all, he was holding the Magic Bottle that he had filched from the defenceless Rabbit's pocket.

The Bottle Rabbit just had time to gasp, 'Stop that. You're a thief. Give me back my Bottle,' when there came a shuffling, scuffling noise and the Crad wasn't there any more. And neither was the Bottle Rabbit's Magic Bottle, his Kindness Prize. The funfair boat moved on (it was pulled along by cables really), trundling past things that were now only mildly frightening, like wailing ghosts, vampires, and tombs that bulged and heaved. The Rabbit, quivering with shock and worry, hardly noticed them. He crouched there, numb, waiting for the trip to end. A last sinister scaffold with a malefactor swinging from it, a last rattle of dry bones, and his boat trundled out into the bright sun again. He blinked dazedly, then leapt out and raced towards Emily.

Emily was looking puzzled. As she'd stood there, expecting the Bottle Rabbit to emerge at any moment, a figure had brushed past her in a dirty raincoat, stalking quickly on awkward feet, untidy, a bit smelly, tall and hunched, with odd bird-like legs and soiled white tennis shoes, the laces undone and trailing. It had been, though she hadn't realized it, the departing Crad, disguised. She had noticed the creature's hectic red eyes, blinking and blinking, and had had a moment of cold dread. Something in the way the creature clutched a small article to itself made her keep on staring at it. She could still see it in the distance, stalking past the big dipper, tall, awkward, clutching.

'Emily, Emily,' gasped the Bottle Rabbit. 'The Crad, it's the Crad again. He's got my . . .' Emily pointed wordlessly in the direction the Crad had taken and the two animals, without another moment's thought, set off after him.

The Crad had stalked past the helter-skelter and the dodgems and had already left the fairground. Normally it would have been impossible for them to keep up with him. But he was still stalking and fluttering along, with odd hops and jumps, like a farmyard hen or duck trying to fly. The fact was that he still had his raincoat on, over his dusty black wings, because the pockets were stuffed with woolly animals, ashtrays, china dogs, penknives and other prizes that he had won at the various shooting ranges. The Crad was an expert shot and was reluctant to relinquish these prizes. So that was why Emily and the Bottle Rabbit were able to keep him in view as he hopped and shuffled out of the funfair, across the car-park, over the highway and the meadows, then into the woods and then further and further into the depths of the forest.

Neither animal spoke as they raced after him, plunging deeper and deeper into the trees, straining to keep that ugly figure in sight. Sometimes he disappeared among tangled branches and dark sunless tree-glooms, but Emily and the Bottle Rabbit were helped in their pursuit by the occasional 'Crark, Crark' that the Crad, apparently unaware of their pursuit, gave triumphant tongue to.

In the densest part of the forest the Crad finally halted before a huge oak tree that had a shabby-looking tree-house ten feet up in its heavy branches. (When she saw it, Emily couldn't help thinking of her own neat little beech-tree home.) The two animals looked at one another, nodded, then crept nearer and nearer, convinced that they were unobserved. The Crad was grimacing and whistling and humming and even singing:

> O won't we 'ave a jolly time
> Drinkin' whisky, beer and wine

and doing a little lopsided hop-step. But suddenly his expression changed into a ferocious glare and, putting his head down, he raced very fast straight at them

where they were crouching behind a bush. His big, balding, pear-shaped head butted. His big beak was wide open. His hectic red eyes blinked and blinked. His clawed feet, yellow and pale and black, tore up the ground. Before they could say 'Jack Robinson' he had a fierce front claw on each of them.

'*Fools*,' he croaked savagely. 'Thought I didn't know yer were after me, didn't yer? *Didn't* yer?' (He shook the Bottle Rabbit quite hard.) 'Well, it's all part of my plan, see? I might just need yer to 'elp me out with the Magic Bottle. *Come* on. *Over* 'ere.' And he dragged the two unfortunate animals towards his oak tree.

In a minute he'd pulled out two sets of handcuffs and the astounded Emily and Bottle Rabbit found themselves manacled to trees twenty yards apart from

85

one another. The Bottle Rabbit's beautiful shining black furry body was squeezed against a silver birch, and Emily's elegant little white cat-body was bound to an elm. The Crad had got hold of some special police handcuffs that were very tight and nasty to have on.

The Crad then half-flew, half-climbed up to his ramshackle tree-house (made of corrugated iron, wire-netting, and plywood). They could hear him unloading his fairground prizes and singing his beer-and-wine song. Then he flopped down again. He'd taken off his raincoat, and they could see all his shaggy, dusty body. Now he was drinking a can of beer and sucking an orange and dropping the orange-peel all over the place. (Emily had already noticed with distaste that the whole area was littered with tins and cans and bottles.) The Crad stared at them both, took a swig of beer, laughed, opened his beak, and began:

'Well, yer do look daft, you two. Makes me laugh, it does. I've got the Bottle and yer can't do nothin' about it, can yer? Well, I mean, *can* yer?' He sneered and laughed in his screeching way. 'Yerss. And don't worry. There won't be no 'angin' about for that big bear friend of yours to throw 'is weight about this time. Forget the bear. And don't worry, there's not goin' to be no Kindness trouble, neither. I got this new Kind friend, see? 'E'll work the Bottle for me. Or 'e'd better if 'e knows what's good for 'im. Yerss. Works down at the post office, Norman does. Kind as any-thin'. You should see Norman with these old animals pickin' up their pensions and that, buyin' special stamps to send to their nephews and stuff. Kind as anythin'. I'd dump the lot of them in the duckpond if it was me, soon as look at 'em. But

Norman's Kind. Yer've never seen anything like it. Yerss. And don't worry, I know the pongles. I been watchin' on the quiet. Didn't know that, did yer? Bet yer didn't. One for sandwiches, two for cold drinks, four for air transport, five for the state-carriage – not that I'd go in for any of that nonsense. Mice in uniform and that. Nigel's the chief one, isn't 'e? I ask you. Nigel.' The Crad gave another sneering cackle. Then he looked irritated again. 'OK, there's other pongles. All right, I don't know 'em all; like there's seven for somethin' or other. But don't worry, these'll keep me goin'. Reckon I'll get them Blue Hares to spill the beans about them others. Didn't think yer could 'old on to that Magic Bottle just for yourself and yer friends, did yer? All yer bloomin' life? What do yer take me for? A idiot?' The Crad laughed uglily and then held up a claw. ''Old it. 'Ere comes Norman now, back from work. Took yer time, didn't yer, Norman?'

While the Crad had been finishing this long, nasty speech a slim, smooth, quite attractive and intelligent-looking pigeon had flown up and landed with a bit of a flourish next to him. He was wearing a French seaman's blue-and-white-striped jersey. The pigeon preened himself, as pigeons do, and smiled at the Crad.

'Well hello hello hel*lo*. Phew. *So* glad to be back, I can't *tell* you. I've never *seen* so many animals in one branch office with tatty *lumpy* brown-paper parcels.' Norman flashed his wide pigeon eyes. 'My dear, you wouldn't *believe* it. Those *crabby* old badgers. *Such* a fuss. Sometimes I just think the post office is *madly* not me. I mean the *noise*, the *people*.' Norman wiped his brow in an elegant way. Then he noticed poor Emily and the Bottle Rabbit.

'Oh, oh. What's this? Naughty naughty. Up to your old badnesses again?' He gave the Crad a little slap.

'Quiet, Norman. Guess what? I've got that Magic Bottle I been tellin' yer about.'

'You *have*? Why, that's simply *marvellous*. What a *clever* old Crad you are. *Do* show me. I'm simply *boiling* with impatience. *Boiling.*'

And in his excitement Norman forgot all about Emily and the Bottle Rabbit, who had to stay chained to their trees while all this went on.

The Crad crarked and crarked and waved the Magic Bottle about, snuffling.

'Just pongle like I tell yer, Norman, and we get food, drink an' transport wherever we bloomin' well want, like I told yer. Look, come over 'ere quick where we can be quiet. And don't forget that Kindness stuff.'

So the Crad and Norman moved off into the bushes. Both Emily and the Bottle Rabbit tried to make reassuring gestures to one another, though it was hard to do, handcuffed as they were. But soon they could hear a familiar sound: creatures trying to make the Magic Bottle work who were not, because of their manifestly unkind behaviour, qualified to do so.

The Crad's voice got loud and angry. 'Why's it not workin', then? You been Kind today, Norman? Not been laughin' at 'unchbacks or anythin', 'ave yer?'

'Can't quite seem to do it,' said Norman. 'There must be some trick to it, dearie. Perhaps it's the way he blinks his eyes. Or perhaps the way he twitches that *divine* little nose of his.'

'Well, you get it straight, Norman. Fast. Or else. Yerss.' The Crad was breathing loudly and menacingly, and clenching and unclenching his claws.

'Oh *come* off it, Craddy. Be reasonable. Don't be

such an old *tyrant*. It's like the Middle *Ages* or something.' Norman smiled at him but the Crad was getting
angrier and angrier. His little red eyes glowed in the
gathering dusk. (It was late afternoon now.) His gnarled legs twitched and his dusty feathers kept lifting and
falling. He muttered something to Norman, glaring
over at the Bottle Rabbit and Emily.

'Oh come *on*, Craddy. Don't be such a *grouch*. They
haven't done us any *harm*, have they? I don't *happen* to
fancy cats much myself; it's just the way I'm made, I
suppose. But that Bottle Rabbit's all right, isn't he?
Quite good-looking, too. Why don't you leave them
alone? Besides, just think about it, Craddy; we're going
to need him for the Bottle *any*way. I just can't quite
seem to catch the *knack* of the absurd thing.'

'Crark, Crark, Crark,' from the Crad. And more
angry muttering.

After a while, Norman came over to the Bottle Rabbit, looking a little embarrassed. 'I say, I do hate all
this, and it's *not* fair on you. And I promise I'll get him
to take off those *vile* handcuffs as soon as poss. But
would you be a dear and give us a hand? Craddy's
getting very peckish, and that does give him such an
awful temper. Could you *bear* to pongle us up a few
sandwiches, lovey?'

'You'll have to shake the Bottle in front of me, then,'
said the Bottle Rabbit in a barely controlled voice. He
was bursting with indignation. And his wrists hurt,
too, and he bet Emily's did as well.

Nevertheless, the resourceful animal had thought of
a plan to outwit the Crad. Norman, with an apologetic
shrug of his elegant shoulders, shook the Bottle for
him, and he quickly pongled up six sandwiches. They
plopped down in front of him, crisp and delicious and

wrapped as usual in freshly-laundered white linen napkins and with the usual little silver knife and little pots of mustard and mayonnaise. The Crad immediately grabbed five sandwiches. 'One'll do yer, Norman. I'm 'ungry.' 'Why, you greedy old thing,' said Norman, 'I'm ashamed of you, really I am.' But the Crad was bolting the sandwiches down, stuffing them wholesale into his beak in a revoltingly greedy way. 'More, more,' he growled. 'Crark, Crark.'

Now the Bottle Rabbit put his plan into action. 'Did you know if you pongle seven times you can get a banquet?' he said timidly. 'Lobster, Turkey à la King, chips, creamed onions, Pêche Melba, everything?'

'Crark, Crark. Do it, then. Quick. What are yer waitin' for? Crark,' said the Crad, licking his lips. 'It'll take about fifteen minutes,' said the Bottle Rabbit. 'What? Well, go on, then,' said the Crad in his surly, impatient way. 'Go ahead. We'll wait.' He paced about. 'Look, Norman. Why don't yer come up and look at my prizes? Come on. I got prizes too, yer know.' He nodded his head at the Bottle Rabbit. 'Yer not the only one, yer know. Come on, Norm. But make 'im get the banquet first.'

Norman, again looking apologetic, smiled at the Bottle Rabbit and shook the Magic Bottle as the Rabbit pongled seven times. Then he and the Crad flew and scrambled up to the Crad's dilapidated tree-house to examine those prizes that the hideous creature had brought back from the funfair.

Of course, what the two of them did not know was that the Bottle Rabbit's seven pongles had alerted the Golden Eagle's All-Day All-Night General Emergency Alarum, and that at that very moment this splendid bird was already beating his way on his powerful wings to this very spot, with his amazing eyes, that could see a thousand miles in any direction, searching and searching.

'Oh, isn't that *lovely*, Craddy. Just lovely? I *adore* this fairground tat. Do let me keep this pink-and-blue plastic kang*aroo*. And yes, I do believe you've won yourself a pink flamingo, too. Yes, you have, you clever old thing you. I *want* it. I *want* it.'

Emily and the Bottle Rabbit could hear Norman carrying on like this, and the Crad grunting and shifting about. And now the Bottle Rabbit saw, with a huge sigh of relief, the great shadow of his friend the Golden Eagle come sweeping across the forest. The wise Eagle gave one little wing-signal and was away again. The Bottle Rabbit knew help was now coming, and tried his best with smiles and nods and shrugs to re-signal the fact to Emily, who, to tell the truth, couldn't make head nor tail of his gestures and grimaces and began to wonder if he'd gone a bit potty under the strain.

But soon a most welcome sound was to be heard. The two persecuted animals knew it of old. THUD, pause. THUD, pause. THUD, pause. Sam the Bear was on his way to the rescue. THUD, pause. Then – SCRASH, pause. SCRASH, pause. Sam was crashing his way through the forest undergrowth and getting nearer and nearer. His great towering body and his great heavy legs, black and huge, were covering yards and yards at a stride. Nothing could stop him.

Now the Crad came flumping down, his face white as a sheet. Norman fluttered after him, clutching his kangaroo and flamingo and looking a little puzzled. ' 'Ere, what's this. What's 'appenin'? Where's me banquet?' said the Crad hoarsely. 'Crark, Crark. I don't

like that row. I hate that 'orrible row.' He was shaking from head to claw and staring out into the forest. And he had good reason to be afraid.

SCRASH, pause, SCRASH. Within minutes Sam the Bear came thundering up and took in the scene at a glance. He was terribly angry. The Bottle Rabbit had never seen him angry like this before.

'How *dare* you manacle these innocent animals in this barbarous fashion?' He picked up the Crad in one paw and shook him till his ugly beak clacked, then threw him from him with a 'Faugh' of disgust. The Crad collapsed in an ungainly heap on the ground. 'Get up, you loathsome creature, and free those hapless animals at once.' Sullenly the Crad crawled over and unhandcuffed Emily and the Bottle Rabbit, who skipped about and rubbed their chafed wrists. 'Thank you, Sam,' they both said. 'Thank you very much.'

Sam the Bear took a few deep breaths to calm himself. 'I'll deal with you in a minute, Crad. Meanwhile, you there, what's your name?' he glared at the slim young pigeon.

'Norman, sir,' said Norman, rather nervously, his clever eyes shifting about.

'Well, you there. Norman, is it? You look like a decent enough sort of young fellow. What makes a young pigeon like you consort with this scoundrelly Crad?'

Norman scratched his head with his plastic flamingo and smiled feebly. 'Oh, well, we're mates, you see? We do lots of things together. I didn't mean any harm,' he grinned.

'Well, I advise you strongly to find other associates in the future.' Sam the Bear had calmed somewhat when he'd seen that Emily and the Bottle Rabbit had not been really hurt, and he settled himself comfortably and began to lay down the law, something he quite liked to do.

'I shall be lenient with you this time, Norman, and let you off lightly.' (Here the Bottle Rabbit quietly asked to speak to him and whispered in his ear about how Norman had tried, in his own way, to protect them from the Crad.) 'Yes, yes, I see, yes,' said Sam the Bear,and went on, 'Now, Norman, you evidently have some good in you. In my view, all this is the result of bad companionship. You should join a respectable social club, Norman. Take up some hobbies. Fretwork, or cycling. Find yourself a nice steady girl-friend.' (Here Norman gave the Bottle

Rabbit a quick wink.) 'Straighten yourself out before it's too late. You only lack direction in life. Determine on some goals and keep them in mind. Now be off with you.'

Then Sam the Bear turned towards the Crad. 'But as for you, Crad, your behaviour has been quite unacceptable. Unacceptable to any civilized group. You'll have to be locked up. Yes. We'll put you in the Stone Barn for a month, on bread and water. Perhaps that will teach you to respect the feelings of other creatures. Society has to be protected from animals like you . . .' Sam the Bear went on like this for some time, while the Crad crouched there, his red eyes snapping and snapping.

Then snorting and hoofbeats were heard, and Fred and Charlie came galloping up, with Count Hubert, the little birthday-rabbit, bouncing up and down and cheering on Charlie's broad back.

'Hurrah! Hurrah!' called Count Hubert, and rushed up to Emily and the Bottle Rabbit and flung his little paws around them. Fred and Charlie looked concerned but pleased. Fred congratulated the Bottle Rabbit on his ruse, and Charlie nodded approvingly. At a word from Sam the Bear, the two cart-horses led the angry Crad off to the Stone Barn. The Crad stalked straight past Norman without so much as a glance.

Norman called after him, 'Well, so long, Craddy. It's been nice knowing you, up to a point. Thanks for the kangaroo and flamingo and sandwich and everything. Be good.' The Crad gave him one baleful look and said nothing as he slumped away between the horses, his dusty feathers ruffled, his gnarled claws twisting and untwisting.

'One of my little mistakes, I suppose,' said Norman,

looking after him and shaking his head. The Bottle Rabbit looked at him rather shyly.

'Norman, how *could* you be friends with that person?'

'Oh I don't know. It was all in fun really.'

'*Fun?*'

'Well, yes. He was so ugly it was wonderful. I mean, I couldn't *believe* he was so ugly.'

The Bottle Rabbit looked puzzled.

'Well yes, dearie,' said Norman, 'I do see how it must have seemed to you. I mean, not a bit funny, I suppose. *Or* kind. But then I love the danger. And nobody liked him. But *no*body.'

'So what are you going to do next?' asked the Bottle Rabbit.

'Me? I'm off south, I think. The warm south. Am I ready for a beakerful of that! Oh boy. I expect I'll drop in and catch some of those piazza-pigeon boys in Venice. That's *my* goal, I think. Then on to Naples. There's some nice rough lads down round the fish-markets there I know, too.' Norman took a little comb out and smoothed the feathers over his forehead. 'Well, goodbye all. See you in church.' And off he flew, clutching his two plastic animals.

'He's an odd sort of bird all right,' said the Bottle Rabbit.

'I don't think he's entirely trustworthy,' said Emily.

'I think he's nice,' said the Bottle Rabbit, meekly. Emily pursed her lips.

Then the whole group walked thoughtfuly back through the forest to Fred and Charlie's cabin. Sam the Bear, who had little Count Hubert on his back, was looking especially thoughtful. He did not like locking anybody up, not even the Crad, and he needed this long stroll to clear his mind. (As a matter of fact, after a couple of days the good-hearted bear, who could not stand the thought of anyone living on bread and water, arranged for the Crad to have ham and salad and cheese brought in, and after about eight days he went down to the Stone Barn and gave the Crad a couple of stern and very lengthy talkings-to, then unlocked the door and let the nasty creature go.)

But today it was still Count Hubert's birthday, so they had a really pleasant party that evening, with dozens of spicy hot-dogs that the little Count kept counting as they bubbled in the pot. He had quite a nice little pile of presents, too. Of course he couldn't stop counting them, so Fred finally had to start opening them for him. It happened, too, that a group of fairground people dropped in later: the Labrador, the Gnu, the Iguana, a whole crowd of talented and witty performing dogs, and no fewer than seven (at least by Count Hubert's count) armadillos, who had just arrived from another hemisphere. The little Count was overjoyed. They all had interesting things to say, and soon the Bottle Rabbit and Emily were able to forget about their extraordinary adventure in the forest, and the Crad in the Horror Room, and the big dipper, and, when bedtime came, were ready enough, like the rest of the company, to drop into a deep sleep. Count Hubert dropped off first as he lay by the fire quite close to the Bottle Rabbit, though they could hear him still dreamily counting: 'One armadillo, eight armadillos, three armadillos, a dugong, nine arma-dillos, sixty-three be-ea-r-s ...' Count Hubert breathed deeply. So did everybody else. And then all was silence in the cosy cabin.

And somewhere, high in the dark sky, the Golden

Eagle was circling and circling, slowly beating his great dark golden wings, keeping a keen eye on them all, watching over them all, making sure that all manner of things would be well.

7

Ken's Little Fling

One day the Bottle Rabbit was strolling by himself again in the woods, coming back from one of his long, quiet walks. It was that midwinter spring season. There had been a brief sun, but the trees were still bare, with all their branches showing and a black, creaky look to them. And everything else had an untidy, soggy, end-of-winter, dark-time-of-year feel: broken twigs and old leaves everywhere, mud underfoot. Yet the Bottle Rabbit could see small shoots of green beginning to show, too, and even the delicate tips of orange, purple and white crocuses glinting under some of the bigger trees. He also noticed that a lot of the birds were back from the south, looking bronzed and fit, chattering and rushing about getting their houses ready for the real spring.

But the Bottle Rabbit shivered. His neat black woolly body couldn't quite keep out the sharp blasts of a wintry east wind that rattled through the forest. It was getting on towards sundown, and the sodden woods were growing dark as well as cold. In the failing light trees took on odd shapes. Some trees looked like trees, of course; but some bushes looked like animals, some even looked like people. One scraggly bush beside a stream looked so much like a person that the Bottle Rabbit almost spoke to it. Then it spoke to *him*, in a crackly, cold voice.

'Hand it over. You don't know me, I expect, but I'm Toad Sister's sister and I haven't much time to waste. Hand it over.'

The Bottle Rabbit gasped in surprise and dismay at these cold words.

'I – I beg your pardon?'

The bush made an impatient gesture with its arms. Of course it wasn't really a bush. It was a weird-looking old woman in a thick black cloak and a tall pointed hat that half-covered a long thin face with a sharp nose and a sharper chin. It struck the Bottle Rabbit that she was not at all unlike the old woman he had once helped over a stream in these very woods, for which he received his Magic Bottle as a Kindness Prize. But this one didn't seem at all generous or even friendly.

'You know what I'm talking about, and *who* I'm talking about,' she screeched. 'My Toad Sister. The one with the toads. There's always half-a-dozen of the little varmints hopping about. Paddocks she calls 'em. She lets 'em get too familiar, in my humble opinion.'

The Bottle Rabbit stood there, puzzled and worried. He was still some way from home and the brief sun was dying. Darkness and cold would soon be completely upon them and there was a touch of menace about this screeching old creature. What was she saying? What was it that she wanted?

She started up again: 'Mind you, she's a good cook, old Toady. Give her that. Makes a first-rate, thick slab-gruel, befuddled old bat that she is. What's she think she's doing, handing out that Bottle to all and sundry? It's not hers to give in the first place, for one thing. So I'll have it back now, thank you very much.'

And with that the old woman stuck out a cold,

99

withered hand from her black cloak and twiddled her fingers impatiently.

'Come on. What are we waiting for?' she screeched again. 'Bottle it is and Bottle it has to be. Hand it over, Rabbit.'

'Well, I call that a bit thick,' burst out the Bottle Rabbit. 'Why should I? What's it got to do with you? She *gave* me my Magic Bottle specially. It's my Kindness Prize. It's mine.'

'Kindness? *Kind*ness?' The old woman laughed loud and long. When she laughed, the tip of her nose nearly met the tip of her chin. 'Listen to him. It's marvellous. Next he'll be saying "Love the little birds," or "Save our bees!" ' She laughed again in her shrill way and then spoke sharply, 'Wake up, Rabbit. Be your age. And *hand over*.' With a sudden strut she was standing over him and staring bleakly into his eyes.

The Bottle Rabbit tried to place a protective paw over the bulging white pocket that contained his Magic Bottle, but he was too late. With a fierce snatch the old woman twitched it out, peered at it, grimaced, and held it up before his eyes. 'Oh no you don't, young Rabbit. Two can play at that game.'

'Wh-what game?' stammered the outraged Bottle Rabbit. 'Give me back my property. You've no right to – ' But even as he spoke the old woman, with a derisive yell, leapt astride what had looked like an ordinary domestic broomstick and hurtled off into the darkening sky. 'Tell that to the birds and bees,' her harsh taunting cry came echoing faintly down.

The Bottle Rabbit stood there staring up at the dwindling figure that was now disappearing with his most prized possession. All this felt like a bad dream.

In fact, he pinched himself to make sure that he was awake. He'd read about animals pinching themselves in books, but it didn't seem to do much good. He was awake all right, and also in a bit of a quandary. He wasn't all that far from Fred and Charlie's cabin, but the trouble was that his two wise and powerful Clydesdale friends were away for the day, competing in a tug of war. Moreover, Emily the Cat, he knew, was back at her own home in the beech tree, and busy with her poker-work. Sam the Bear was off playing indoor tennis all day. The Golden Eagle was attending yet another high-speed bird conference. Even the fun-fair people had all left town, and although the Golden Baker had said he might drop in some time that evening with some freshly-baked pies and buns as a present, there was no knowing with him when he would turn up. The poor Bottle Rabbit had no one to help him.

But as he started plodding wearily homewards, he all at once heard a trotting sort of twinkling and rustling in the dead leaves, and,

'Having a bit of trouble, old man?'

The Bottle Rabbit started and looked round. Standing there was a plumpish, rather good-looking pig, in tweed jacket, flat tweed cap and heavy brogues. He held a natty-looking little leather-bound cane tight under his left front oxter. The pig winked confidently at the Bottle Rabbit.

'Why, it's you, Ken, isn't it?' cried the Bottle Rabbit happily. The plump pig nodded and grinned.

Now it was true that the Bottle Rabbit had had various uncertain dealings with Ken in the past. More than once this less-than-straightforward pig had tried to lead him down the garden path and filch his precious Bottle from him (only to be thwarted by the Bottle Rabbit's close friends, notably Sam the Bear). Yet there was something very likeable about Ken the Pig, and the Bottle Rabbit had always got on well with him. And he was certainly very glad to see him now.

'What's wrong then, old man?' said Ken.

'I've – I've lost my Bottle – had it taken away.'

'What, again? I must say, old man, you do seem to . . . Who was it *this* time, then?'

'Well, there was this old woman . . .'

'Not another of *them*, old man? You do let these old biddies muck you about, don't you? So what happened *this* time?'

The Bottle Rabbit told him. Ken nodded, shook his head, whistled a bit, flicked his whangee at a nettle and, settling down on a tree-stump, started to file his nails. As he looked at Ken, the Bottle Rabbit realized, with extreme interest, that he was wearing a wig.

'A bit of a tall order, this one, old man,' Ken mused. 'Those old sisters are a weird lot, I can tell you that.'

'I *know*,' said the Bottle Rabbit.

'I don't know about those sisters,' said Ken. 'We kick the topic around, me and the boys, down at the club, now and then, over a few drinks. I mean, they keep fiddling about all day and all night with their charms and spells and toads and mumbo-jumbo – the whole bag of tricks. But what's it all add up to? I'll tell you what, old man – when push comes to shove they can't cut the mustard, old man. None of them can't.' He looked at the Bottle Rabbit triumphantly.

'How do you mean, mustard?' said the Bottle Rabbit.

'I mean they don't *achieve*, old man,' said Ken patiently. 'No know-how. No clout.'

'Clout?'

'I'll grant you she's got that broomstick,' went on Ken. 'Well, fair enough. I'll grant you that, old man. They do have travel capability. But what odds? The plain fact is, that's not enough these days. I mean, where does it get them, old man? I ask you.'

'I don't know,' said the Bottle Rabbit.

'Look, I'll let you into my secret, old boy. The secret of my methods. The secret of my success.' Ken the Pig looked round carefully and drew closer to the Bottle Rabbit. He put a trotter up to the Rabbit's ear and in a controlled whisper said, 'Psychology of the individual, old man. Works like a charm. Psychology of the individual. Works every time.' He drew back and nodded several times.

'Really?' said the Bottle Rabbit.

'So all we need to do is get the old – is to have her fly back here, with the Bottle, of course, and get cracking, using the you-know-what. Problem is – how do we get her back?'

The Bottle Rabbit thought for a bit, then:

'Perhaps I could write her a letter and explain how it really is my Bottle,' he said.

Ken looked at him for some time without saying anything.

'But then, how could I? I don't know her address,' said the Bottle Rabbit.

Ken looked at him some more.

'Pity, that,' he said at last. 'That's a real pity.' Ken put his nail file away. 'Look, let's sit down. There's a little shelter over by those yew trees, old man. Let's take the weight off our feet. The light's going and it's getting a bit nippy. I'll do us a fire.' And Ken led the cold, tired, unhappy Rabbit over to the shelter and sat him down. Then, with a few deft movements, the pig built a little fire of twigs and branches. Producing a fat, shiny, chromium-plated cigarette lighter he soon had it crackling away. 'That's more like it,' said Ken. 'Now, how about a drop of what the doctor ordered?' He pulled out a silver hip-flask. 'Go on. Be my guest. Take a good swig. The best brandy money can buy, this is. Australian, you know. No expense spared.'

The Bottle Rabbit obediently took a big gulp. The strong spirits coursed through his furry body, and he gave Ken a grateful grin.

'Warms up your insides in no time, doesn't it, old man? Just the job,' said Ken, and he took a swig himself. The pig was thinking very fast now. 'Tell you what, old man. You look a bit fagged. Why don't you doss down here for a little shut-eye and leave things to me. OK?'

'Well, I *am* a bit sleepy after that brandy.'

'So curl up next to the fire. Take forty winks, old man.'

And this is what the Bottle Rabbit did. Meanwhile, Ken was saying to himself: 'She'll be back any minute. Bound to be. She can't make the thing work any more than the rest of 'em. So what'll I do? What's my line going to be?' He bit off the end of a big cigar, lit it, paced up and down, and sat down again.

'I could chat her up, I suppose.' Ken puffed on his cigar and twirled an imaginary long curly moustache. 'No. What am I saying? No, no. It's not on, old man, not really.' He buffed his nails and flicked fluff off his jacket. 'Mind you, nothing like a bit of the old soft soap in the end. Anyway, we'll wait and see. Shouldn't be long now.'

He was right. In no time at all came a whoosh and a whirr, and standing in front of him was a little old woman with a conical hat and black cloak, a long nose and a pointed chin. Numerous small red-eyed creatures hopped and fluttered and wriggled around her. Ken immediately threw away his cigar, sprang to his feet, and bowed low from the waist. He removed his flat tweed cap and swept the ground with it in a twirling flourish.

'All hail, great Queen. May your life be as prosperous and bright as sunrise on a clear day,' bellowed Ken.

The old woman looked a bit surprised, but seemed ready to answer him. 'What wind has brought you hither?' she screeched.

'I come a-wooing,' Ken roared. ('Might as well give it the old try,' he said to himself.) 'Let not this simple garb deceive you. I am not as ordinary pigs. I am an enchanted pig from the north. Vouchsafe me but your hand and some small token of your love (may I suggest that small green Bottle you've got there) and all my treasure will be at your command: marble halls, vassals and serfs, riches too great to count, – 'ere, what are you laughing at?' said Ken.

'Come a-wooing? Give *you* the Bottle? Listen, you've got it wrong, young fellow. I'm Toad Sister, not that pinhead who just grabbed the Bottle from the kind Rabbit. You've got it all mixed up.' The old woman now laughed very heartily. When she laughed, the tip of her nose nearly met the end of her chin. 'I'm bringing his Bottle *back* to him, see? Get it? I gave that sister a piece of my mind, I can tell you, poking her nose in where she's not wanted. She won't do that again in a hurry, believe you me. You're Ken the Pig, aren't you? I've heard about you. Now where's that young Rabbit?'

Ken, speechless for once, pointed to where the Bottle Rabbit lay dozing. The pig was deeply embarrassed; he felt a bit of a fool in fact.

'Seems a pity to wake him up,' said the old woman. 'Nothing like a nap. Look, I'm in a hurry. It's Candlemas Eve, you know, a busy night for us sisters.' She cackled. 'Just give him his Bottle back when he wakes up. No tricks, mind. Come on, toads.' And she leapt on to her broomstick. 'Well, look after yourself, Ken. What was it again? "Marble halls?" You *are* a caution, and no mistake. "Vouchsafe me but your hand." Wait till I tell the sisters that one.' The old woman laughed and laughed, and shot off into the sky.

Ken was thoroughly discomfited. 'Made a proper butcher's shop of that one, didn't I?' he said to himself. He was really fed up. Yet as he thought over what the old woman had screeched at him, he couldn't help starting to grin a bit. 'I am not as ordinary pigs,' he murmured to himself, smiling. 'Pretty good, that.' Then he looked longingly at the Magic Bottle in his hand, glanced over at the sleeping Rabbit, had an idea, and immediately brightened up. 'Of course I'll give him back his Bottle in the end,' he murmured. 'Of course I will. But what if I borrow it for a week or two first?' The pig nodded his head. 'He couldn't really mind, could he? After all, I've been being pretty kind, for me. And he could manage without it for six months or so.' Ken turned away and took a step into the yew trees, between the live and the dead nettles. 'And I can always get it back to him next year, or maybe the year after. Yes. Why not?' He took a few more steps. 'Well, so long, Bottle Rabbit old man.' And he trotted rather hesitantly away.

But then he looked back at the sleeping Bottle Rabbit, curled up with his paws folded over his stomach, calm and trusting. Ken set his face firmly at the woods and moved on, gripping the Magic Bottle tight in one trotter. Then he looked back yet again and wearily he shook his head. There was, after all, much good in this pig. Yet the Bottle meant a great deal to him, too. So then Ken had one more idea. Perhaps he could get the Bottle Rabbit to lend it to him for a bit? and then, who knows? He sighed, straightened himself, trotted slowly back, bent down and gently shook the Bottle Rabbit awake.

'What? What's this?' The Rabbit sat up and rubbed his eyes with both paws.

'Bottle Rabbit, look what I've won back for you,' said Ken, eyeing him sharply.

'What is it? What did you win? Oh, my *Bottle*! Oh thank you, Ken. Thank you very much,' said the Rabbit sleepily. 'Wonderful! But how on earth did you manage it?'

Ken coughed modestly. 'Well, it was a long struggle. A battle, actually. I didn't mind their toads and their beetles, old man; I could deal with them with one hand tied behind my back – '

'Then you didn't use the psychology of the whatsisname?'

'No time, old man, no time. They came at me from behind, do you see? It was their nasty bats nearly did for me; but I've peppered two of them, I'm sure of that. I've escaped by a miracle, to tell you the truth, old man.'

'Good Lord,' said the Bottle Rabbit.

Ken coughed again. 'But no more of that, old man. All in the day's work. The least I could do for a pal.'

Now Ken winced and began to limp rather heavily.

'What's wrong?' said the Rabbit. 'You didn't get hurt fighting for my Bottle, did you?'

'Oh, no, no, *no*. Nothing to worry about. It's just that this silly old leg of mine got it when that damn great bat came at me.'

The Bottle Rabbit looked horrified.

'By the bye, old man.' Ken winced again and coughed again, glancing at the Rabbit with his shrewd eyes. He was still holding the Bottle, and now his little tail began to twiddle very fast. 'I don't suppose you could see your way to letting me have the old Bottle for a day or two? Just by way of a loan, you know? Between good pals? I could let you have it back next month or the month after? Or early next year? Fact is, I'm a bit short just now and I could do with a – a – a –'

Ken broke off, stammering, and then started talking very fast. 'Well, glad to have been of service, old boy. Any time. Just say the word. Just call on me. Just ask for Ken. Be my – Hello, Sam. I'm just leaving.' Ken's light blue eyes were now staring fixedly over the Bottle Rabbit's shoulder at none other than Sam the Bear, who had come up quietly behind the Rabbit. Sam was wearing a white woolly sweater and white shorts and was carrying a tennis racquet under one powerful muscular arm. He had just come from practice at the Bears' Winter Gymnasium.

'Well, well, Ken. Jolly glad to see you. I've just met and exchanged a few words with an acquaintance of yours, that extraordinary old Toad Sister. She seems to think quite a lot of you. It appears that you have been of the utmost service to our young friend here.' Sam patted the Bottle Rabbit on the head as he spoke. 'Just

giving him his Bottle back now, eh? Jolly good. Good work, Ken. Keep it up.'

Sam smiled broadly as Ken handed the Bottle back to the rather dazed Rabbit, who was still not fully awake after his little brandy-snooze.

'Not going, are you, Ken?' said Sam.

'Got to be shoving off now,' Ken said glumly. 'So long, Bottle Rabbit old man. Reckon it just isn't my day, somehow. Well, keep fit. Toodle-oo all.'

Sam nodded at the pig benignly. 'Digs all right, are they, Ken?' he called after him. 'Very important, that. That and a well-balanced diet. Good. Jolly good.'

Sam watched as Ken trotted off into the dark woods. 'Splendid pig, that, in many ways,' said Sam. 'Not wholly commendable, of course, but he has a peculiar genius of his own.' He paused as Ken's distant voice wound through the trees, once more raised in song. Not a pig-brag this time, nor precisely a lament, yet a song with all the deep melancholy of pig-wandering and pig-wonder in it:

> All things have rest, why should *we* toil alone?
> *We* only toil, who are the first of things,
> And make perpetual moan,
> Still from one sorrow to another thrown,
> Nor ever fold pigs' wings . . .

Ken's voice died away. The little fire had gone out now. All was dark and still. Sam the Bear took the Bottle Rabbit's small paw in his huge one and they picked their way carefully back to the cabin in the odd, thick darkness of a February night.

At Fred and Charlie's cabin, lights were gleaming and rich chimney-smoke told them that a good fire was already lit. The Golden Baker had just cycled up with a big batch of steaming hot steak-and-kidney pies and freshly baked currant buns. The two Clydesdales, who had won an Honourable Mention in the tug of war, were safely home and already celebrating by mulling up some big porcelain jugs of wine. So everybody settled down to munch and gulp round the fire. And all evening long, various good animal friends appeared and joined the peaceful, cheerful party.

Now it was getting late and it was time to sleep. All grew quiet as they sat watching the fitful flames and listening to the east wind rattling down the chimney. 'Candlemas Eve,' murmured Fred, at last breaking the late-night silence. 'Lots of strange creatures abroad; some queer things moving about outside tonight. It's good to be warm and peaceful at home.' The Bottle

Rabbit, half-hearing in the stillness, smiled sleepily to himself and patted his Magic Bottle. He was quietly hoping that Ken the Pig was also warm and happy somewhere. 'Yes, Candlemas Eve,' went on Fred. 'Real spring can't be far off now.' Charlie nodded, and other sleepy animals mumbled in agreement as they all dozed off peacefully round the glowing logs.